A LITTLE BIT OF CHRISTMAS MAGIC

As a wedding planner at Carrick Park Hotel, Ailsa McCormack is organising a Christmas Day wedding at the expense of her own holiday. Not that she minds. She's always been fascinated by the place and its past occupants; particularly the beautiful and tragic Ella Carrick, whose striking portrait still hangs at the top of the stairs. And then an encounter with a tall, handsome and strangely familiar man in the drawing room on Christmas Eve sets off a chain of events that transforms Ailsa's lonely Christmas into a magical occasion . . .

Books by Kirsty Ferry
in the Linford Romance Library:

EVERY WITCH WAY
SUMMER AT CARRICK PARK

KIRSTY FERRY

A LITTLE BIT OF CHRISTMAS MAGIC

Complete and Unabridged

LINFORD
Leicester

First published in Great Britain in 2017

First Linford Edition
published 2019

*A catalogue record for this book is available
from the British Library.*

ISBN 978–1–4448–4192–3

Published by
F. A. Thorpe (Publishing)
Anstey, Leicestershire

Set by Words & Graphics Ltd.
Anstey, Leicestershire
Printed and bound in Great Britain by
T. J. International Ltd., Padstow, Cornwall

This book is printed on acid-free paper

To my family, who make every Christmas special!

Acknowledgements

Thank you to my wonderful publishers Choc Lit, who have allowed me the indulgence of my very first Christmas book. Fortunately, I managed to write it over the Christmas season, but my poor editor had to do her work during the summer months, so I do apologise if the thought of mince pies and ice-skating jarred with sunny days and ice creams! Thanks must go to her, and the rest of the team who made this possible — to the super Tasting Panel who read it and enjoyed it, to my wonderful cover designer and to my gorgeous Choc Lit family, who understand the doubt and insecurity of the writing life and are always there for a chat or a pep talk. Special thanks to Catherine L, Melissa B, Claire W, Sigi, Lucy M, Jo O, Jennifer S, Sarah B-H, Barbara P, Susan D, Anne E, Dimi,

Rachel D, Carol F and Cordy S who passed the manuscript on the Panel.

Thanks must also go to the readers who loved the 'Rossetti Mysteries' series and asked me to write more about the people they had come to love. Ella and Adam are very special characters to me — they were the first ones to keep me awake at night whilst they told me their story, and I felt they deserved more than simply being a part of *Some Veil Did Fall*. This book is for them, and for everybody who believes that angels can come to us in the strangest of guises; but especially when we need them most.

'We hear the Christmas angels . . . '

O Little Town of Bethlehem:
A Christmas Carol

1

Christmas Present

'I don't know who would choose to get married on Christmas Day,' said Tara, the Carrick Park receptionist. 'It's just an odd day to get married. Most people would choose Christmas Eve, surely? Much nicer. And they don't miss out on presents or Christmas dinner then.'

Ailsa McCormack shook her head. 'It's their choice,' she said. As the Wedding Events Coordinator at Carrick Park Hotel, she was used to all sorts of foibles and requests from brides, grooms and anything in between; but she had to admit that even she hadn't organised a wedding for Christmas Day before.

'You're going to have a very early start tomorrow, aren't you?' asked Tara sympathetically.

'I am.' Ailsa sighed and looked around

her at the decorations in the entrance hall. There was a huge Christmas tree in the alcove by the grand staircase, elegantly covered with silver and blue decorations and a fire was roaring and crackling in the large fireplace, garlands of greenery swathed over the mantelpiece.

The heady smell of pine resin and wood smoke seemed as familiar to this place as the salt-tinged breezes that swept across the North Yorkshire moors and embraced the old building. Carrick Park had been, once upon a time, the home of the Carrick family, but had, eventually, become a hotel when the last owner, Lydia Carrick, had sold it.

''Change the name and not the letter, marry for worse and not for better',' murmured Ailsa, her eyes drifting to a bookshelf built into the alcove nearby.

'Who are you thinking of?' asked Tara curiously, leaning forwards at her desk.

'Lydia Carrick. She married her cousin Jacob, didn't she? Somewhere along the line they made sure the

Carrick name continued so one of the husbands had to take his wife's name to ensure the inheritance — so they were both Carricks. And if the *letter* makes for a bad marriage, God help the person who marries someone of the same name!'

Lydia Carrick's cousin, Jacob, had, apparently been the undoing of everything the family held dear; the instigator of the disaster of Lydia's marriage; the subsequent unravelling of Carrick Park as the family home — the man who, too tragically, had loved Lady Eleanor Carrick to distraction and hated Adam, Lydia's brother, because Eleanor — or Ella, as she was known — had loved Adam instead.

'Ah! That's all in the book, isn't it?' Tara nodded across to the bookshelf. It held a well-thumbed copy of a book about the family who had lived at Carrick Park, and more hardback copies were piled neatly on a unit nearby for visitors to purchase. 'And don't forget the ghosts!'

'Ghost in the singular,' said Ailsa with a grin. 'There's only supposed to be Ella here, Lydia's sister-in-law.'

The book Tara referred to had been written by Becky Nelson, a journalist who had caused quite a storm with an article she had published about a famous painting. Before that, her Carrick Park book had detailed the mystery of Ella and Adam Carrick's sudden disappearance in 1865. Lydia had inherited the house after that, but had moved out of the place just as soon as she could.

Becky suggested that Ella and Adam had been caught in a thunderstorm, and there had been a terrible accident. Jacob had been the sole witness, and had taken most of the secrets of that night to his grave.

There was a beautiful Landseer portrait of Ella on the staircase, displaying her formal title of Lady Eleanor Carrick. Ella's tragic spirit was supposed to drift around the hotel and play the piano, but Ailsa had never seen her or heard her. Neither had Rosa, the Senior Receptionist. The fact that Ella played the piano at all was a story in itself, as she had apparently lost her hearing when she was quite young.

'I'm sure the piano was going the other day,' said Tara, raising her eyebrows. 'I'm sure I heard Christmas carols.' A piano had been reinstated in the old drawing room, which had, up until a couple of years ago, been the hotel restaurant and bar.

The management had since decided that the space served better as a function room, and during an almighty refurbishment, the restaurant was relocated to the morning room, the bar moved into the study and the newer dividing walls knocked down again, as the drawing room was opened back up to its full size. Ailsa preferred the new layout; it was much better for weddings and, in her opinion, reflected more the character of the original Carrick Park, which was something she cared deeply about. Her working environment was one reason why she loved her job so much.

They'd all joked at the time of the building work that ghosts didn't like refurbishments and it usually stirred things up with them. Ailsa had hoped, just quietly to herself, that Ella might materialise out of the plaster and rubble and shake an elegant fist at them for messing up her home — but she hadn't, leaving Ailsa slightly disappointed.

Today, though, Ailsa laughed. 'Don't play the innocent with me, Tara. It's Mozart Ella plays — not Christmas carols.'

Tara smiled. 'I'm rumbled. Just teasing.'

'Well don't bother,' replied Ailsa, good-humouredly. She picked up her iPad and hugged it to her. 'I've still got some work to do for tomorrow, so I'll head into the office and get onto it. Do you want anything while I'm on my travels? Coffee? Tea? One of Rosa's mince pies?'

Tara groaned. 'I can't eat any more of

those pies. I've had three today already. I'll just sit here and think about what I'm missing at home — like stress and panic and erratic tempers.'

'Families, eh? Mine are scattered all over now. Meanwhile — ' Ailsa raised the iPad. 'I have to sort out a wedding.'

'Good luck. Are you staying here overnight then?'

'Might as well.' Ailsa sighed. 'I normally go to Edinburgh for Christmas, but — ' she put on a broader Scottish accent than she actually possessed,' — it's nae gonna happen this year is it? Never mind.'

It wasn't too much of a hardship to stay at Carrick Park this year. Ailsa had been brought up by her Aunt Moira and Uncle Stewart after her parents had died, but this year, they were heading to Australia to spend Christmas with their son. One of her other cousins had just recently put roots down in the borders and married a girl from Jedburgh and her other cousin had moved to Derbyshire. Ailsa wasn't quite sure where she fitted in any more, which was silly really as she was an adult and had been established in Yorkshire since she finished university. But still; it felt a bit odd not having her relatives around her at this time of the year.

'At least you'll have a bit of company tonight if you're here,' said Tara. 'I'll be around until one in the morning — then Louisa will be here until nine. And Rosa's coming in after that to work the day shift.'

'Well I hope Joel's making her dinner for when she gets in!' commented Ailsa. 'She'll be ready for it.'

'He's bound to. She's got him well trained.'

'Good for her.'

'Do you know,' said Tara, looking thoughtful, 'I'm really surprised this couple you're looking after got anyone on board to sort out a wedding for Christmas Day.'

'People have businesses to run,' replied Ailsa. 'They'll charge extra, no doubt, but I don't suspect many of them would turn down the chance of a job. And speaking of businesses, I must get off and do this. See you!'

'Have fun!' called Tara as Ailsa headed off to the office. It was at the back of Carrick Park, part of the old servants' quarters and had possibly been a housekeeper's room or a butler's pantry at one point; but clearly it had been nicely refurbished as an office space and Ailsa managed to get through her bits and pieces with the help of another cup of tea and a shortbread biscuit.

It was about ten-thirty when she finally closed down the iPad and rubbed her eyes. She didn't keep standard hours at the best of times but this was altogether different. She couldn't refuse Sophie and Gabe, the bride and groom, their special day; but part of her wondered if they'd done it so the anniversary date was easier to recall. She'd found out that Gabe's birthday was on Christmas Day too. She smiled at the thought, mentally scolded herself for even supposing that and left the empty office to the whir of the cooling fans in the computers and the gentle hum of electrics.

In the olden days, this place would have been crawling with people — all these bells, for instance, along the corridor would have been destined to ring for whatever reason. It wasn't the first time she'd considered that and she looked at the faded, painted labels by each one as she passed: *Blue Bedroom, Nursery, Drawing Room . . .*

The drawing room. Her favourite room in the whole building. It was, it seemed, the perfect evening and the perfect time to go in and spend a little time in that drawing room to wind down before bed. She was officially off-shift, so it couldn't be classed as loitering — and besides, that was the room Sophie and Gabe had booked for tomorrow, so it was maybe just as well that she go in and just check it over. Or so she told herself, anyway.

★　★　★

Ned walked around the drawing room, seeing the old room brought back to life after the refurbishment. This was better. This was how it was meant to be. It had never looked right before — no way would the Carricks have had a bar in their drawing room, let alone dining tables.

No, the Carrick Park dining room was the only place they would take their meals, and all that ever got served in the drawing room were pots of tea and the occasional sandwich or cake. At Christmas, the servants would have brought mulled wine and mince pies, of course, and Lydia had still liked, sometimes, to warm her mulled wine the traditional way by using a poker and putting it in the glass after she'd left it in the fire for a little while. It wasn't such a good idea, though, when she got bits of ash in her wine, and complained of it having a distinctly smoky flavour, when the rest of them were wrapping their hands around glasses which had been brought from the kitchen, already full of warm, spicy, plum-coloured liquid, heated in a big copper pan on the hob.

Ned smiled. Lydia had been one of a kind. He looked at the book he had thumbed through earlier and was pleased to see that Becky Nelson had done such an excellent job of telling their stories — telling Ella's story, in particular. In his mind's eye, he saw the Landseer on the staircase and, despite everything that had happened, he could still spare a thought for Ella Dunbar and the fact that she had been forever captured as Lady Eleanor Carrick. She would have hated the formality of it.

The book had even said that, despite her sense of humour and the confidence she had within her immediate circle, she was quite shy when she was out of her comfort zone. Becky Nelson was correct. If you couldn't hear anything that was going on around you, how could you hope to react appropriately to something that might throw you? Ella had been completely deaf for some time before she married Adam. You had to admire her. She tried. Goodness only knew, she'd tried. It was a crying shame that her stubbornness had been the catalyst for all that had happened, but you couldn't change the past and that was the God honest truth.

The door clicked behind him and Ned turned. A slim, dark-haired girl came into the room clutching an iPad. His heart skipped a beat and he couldn't help but smile. She had pale, creamy-coloured skin which he knew would boast a dusting of freckles over her nose in the summer and the most beautiful brown eyes he had seen for a long time. They were probably the same hue as a fresh horse chestnut, and just as enticing. Her hair was loose and bounced around below her shoulders in waves, the ends kinking up, not quite tamed.

'Good evening,' he said, thinking he'd better let her know he was in there. 'Sorry — do you need to lock up?

I was just enjoying some peace and quiet.'

'Oh!' The girl started. She had a good right. He had been hidden in the shadows behind the piano, only stepping out of them as he spoke. 'No. No, it's fine. I'm not here to lock up. My excuse is that I'm checking it for a wedding tomorrow — Gabe and Sophie? You might know them — you might be a guest! Sorry — I feel as if we should have been introduced already?' She blinked, clearly more puzzled than he was.

'Ah, Gabe and Sophie,' agreed Ned. 'Because Gabe's birthday falls around Christmas time, hence his name.'

'Exactly. I'm Ailsa McCormack, the Wedding Events Coordinator for Carrick Park. I'm just doing some last-minute work, making sure it's all perfect for them.'

She held out her hand and Ned took it, shaking it and marvelling at how warm it was compared to his. 'I'm sure it will be,' he replied with a smile. 'But I bet I know what you're going to grumble about.'

'Oh? Do I have a grumbling sort of face on me?' asked Ailsa, tilting her head and looking amused.

'I didn't say that,' said Ned, laughing. Her accent was perfect — soft and Scottish, with a smile in every word. 'I think you're going to say you wish they'd put the Christmas tree in the middle of this room, instead of the foyer.'

'You read my mind! Yes, I always say I think it'll look better in there, but I keep getting told it would disrupt too much if they did that. I'm sure they think you'd have Gabe going around one side of it and Sophie going around the other when they walked back up the aisle. Plus, it would be in the way for the reception.'

'Do you think this is where it would have been when the Carricks were here?' asked Ned.

'I'm almost certain,' replied Ailsa, 'but all that's lost to history now. I see you've got a copy of their book.' She nodded towards his hand, as he clutched the hardback. 'What do you think?'

'I think I'm inclined to agree with you. I'm Edward Cavendish, by the way. I'm very pleased to meet you, Ailsa McCormack.'

'Edward Cavendish?' Ailsa frowned for a moment. 'I can't recall the name, but they've got so many guests. You do seem very familiar, though. I've seen people coming and going all day — that's probably it.'

'Probably. I might be there as Ned. I often get that instead. So is it all right for me to be in here, then? You don't need me shifted out?'

'Not unless you're planning on falling asleep on one of the sofas, then I think the night porters might get a bit concerned. It wouldn't have been the first time we found a guest napping in here, though. It's very cosy.'

'I love the open hearth,' he said, moving towards it. He put the book down on a coffee table and leaned over, rubbing his hands together in the warmth. 'I doubt it would heat the whole room though. It's a big space.'

'Yes, but it's much nicer since they revamped the Park and knocked the two rooms into one again. It just looks better. I love the piano.' Ailsa nodded towards it. 'I bet it got a bit chilly over there, though, away from the fireplace!'

'Well perhaps it wasn't always there,' suggested Ned. 'Look — I've got a bottle of wine here.' He nodded to one of the tables by the fire. 'Can I prevail upon you to share it with me? Once you're finished work, of course. We can chat about the old-fashioned Carrick Park. Try to establish which room was which, that kind of thing. I love old places and history.'

'Oh.' Ailsa looked a little thrown. 'I'm very tempted. I officially finished work about three hours ago, to be honest, but I've just been hanging around and finishing bits and bobs off since then. I'm staying here tonight — it's just easier than going home if I've got to be here early in the morning anyway. Perk of the job. But you've only got one glass.'

'That's easily resolved,' said Ned. He looked at the door. 'It would be good if they still had bell-pulls, wouldn't it? As it is, I'll nip out and ask the girl on reception.'

'Tara. Her name's Tara,' replied Ailsa. 'But it's fine, I can go and get one — '

'No, I wouldn't dream of it. You sit down, you've been working. I've been lounging around most of the evening. I'll go. I won't tell her it's for you. She might get jealous that you can relax and she can't.'

Ailsa laughed. 'Good plan. Okay.' She smiled at him. 'I'll wait here.'

'I won't be long,' promised Ned. He looked at her as she sat down by the fireplace and a smile curved his lips. She was lovely. Absolutely lovely.

He'd known her straight away.

2

Ailsa sat down and watched the man — Ned — walk out of the room, long-legged and well-toned. Even his back view was pretty nice.

The strangest thing was, that she definitely felt she already knew Ned. At first, she had thought he was part of Gabe's entourage; someone she must have seen with the bridegroom-to-be on one of his visits to the hotel. But as she talked to him, she realised it was a different sort of recognition — she was no psychologist, but she knew the innermost workings of a person's mind could create all sorts of situations; and it seemed that this man had been dredged out of *her* innermost workings and brought to life, somehow, before her.

For years, she'd had fractured dreams of someone who looked just like this Ned did — tall, dark-haired, pale-skinned and altogether a pretty nice package. He was never quite clear in the dreams, though, apart from his eyes, which were always dark and seemed to drill right into her heart. She largely put the dreams down to the fact that she worked, day-in, day-out with loved-up couples — and if anyone had ever asked her what her ideal man looked like she would answer without hesitation: 'tall, dark and hand-some'. It was such a cliché, but it was true. Ailsa had always been attracted to dark-haired men. And if that was her only vice, dreaming about a man who may or may not exist, then so what? Ned was certainly up there with the best of them.

It had to be a psychological thing, it had to be. He was a lot like the man she dreamed about, but people generally didn't step out of your dreams and into your life, did they? No. It had to be a combination of things; she was attracted to men that looked like Ned, she dreamed about men who looked like Ned, and Ned — well — he obviously *looked* like

Ned and it was the overall *impression* of Ned that sparked that strange little jolt of recognition. The subconscious mind was a powerful thing.

His face was so pale and his dark eyes were such a contrast it had been difficult to drag her own gaze away from them. She'd had the sense he'd felt a similar pull — but maybe that was just wishful thinking. One of her brides had once told her she just 'clicked' with her partner and Ailsa had always wondered about that — whether such a thing could happen or not. Ned was most definitely something different and she already decided that she liked him, even in the brief few minutes they had spent together. Or maybe it was just a little bit of harmless lust and/or flirtation at the end of a very long day. All she had wanted to do was flop into bed after her patrol of the drawing room, but now it didn't seem like too much of a chore to spend a little bit of time here on Christmas Eve and just absorb the magic that was and always had been Carrick Park.

'Here we go.' The door opened and Ned walked in with an extra glass. 'She didn't ask too many questions, but I could see it in her eyes. I must look furtive.'

'Furtive. That's a good word,' said Ailsa. 'She'll give me an inquisition next time I see her — fraternising with the wedding guests and such like. But hey — all I have to tell her is we were discussing Carrick Park. She might think I was drumming up business.'

'She might,' replied Ned. He poured her a drink and handed her the glass. 'Merry Christmas,' he said, raising his own.

'Merry Christmas!' she replied. She took a sip of the wine and settled back in the seat. 'It's a shame it's not mulled. It would have been nice for Christmas Eve.'

'I think they used to put pokers in their glasses to stir them up. Maybe we should try that for you?' Ned made a big show of getting a poker and putting it in the flames. He looked up at her quizzically, the golden and red shadows burnishing his slightly stubbled cheeks.

'No thanks. Knowing my luck, I'd shatter the glass with the heat. Then I'd spend half the night picking up bits of glass so people don't hurt themselves tomorrow. And that would be my relaxing Christmas Eve finished before it had even started.'

'That's *your* luck, though. Here, let me do it. I promise it won't shatter and if it does, I'll pick it up, okay?'

Ailsa shook her head and laughed. 'If you can promise me you'll not damage anything, then go for it. But we haven't got any spices in it, so it can't be proper mulled wine, can it?'

'Let me work a little bit of Christmas magic,' said Ned with a smile. 'I guarantee it'll taste like the proper stuff after I've finished. May I?' He held the poker up and raised his eyebrows.

'Go on then.' Ailsa could feel the giggles bubbling up as she held the glass out.

Sure enough, Ned put the poker in and stirred the liquid very carefully. 'There we go. Try that.'

'All right.' Ailsa smiled, sceptical, and tilted the glass to her lips. To her surprise, she tasted a warm, spicy liquid, with definite hints of cinnamon and cloves. 'Ooh,' she said. 'That *is* nice.'

'Maybe it's the power of suggestion, maybe it's magic,' said Ned with a grin. 'Or maybe, perhaps more likely, it's just what that brand of red tastes like.' He heated the poker up again and did the same to his own drink. 'Mmm, that *is* good. And not a hint of ash.' He held the poker up and studied it. 'It is *truly* magical.'

Ailsa felt the warmth of the wine travel down into her tummy and smiled over the top of the glass. Those eyes! He was staring right at her and she felt her cheeks burn up a little; which might, of course, have been the effect of the alcohol.

She tore her gaze away and looked

into the flames. 'They don't usually leave pokers and things near the fires,' she mused. 'Maybe they were trying for a bit of atmosphere in here. I'm not complaining.'

'Best not to mention it,' replied Ned. He replaced the poker in the brass bucket next to the fire and sat back in his seat. 'Talking of bell-pulls, have they still got the old bells down in the corridors? I've been here lots of times, but I have to say I've never really been down there — obviously! I suspect there's not much reason for guests to be down there — but I know in a lot of these places they keep them as a curiosity.'

'Oh, they're still there. I pass them all the time. The offices are down that way. If it's late at night and I'm on my own, I must confess I run past them. I just think what would happen if one of them rang? I'd probably run straight out of the back door. There's a courtyard out there and it says in that book there used be a fountain in the middle of it.'

'Oh yes — the angel fountain.' Ned

nodded thoughtfully. 'I bet that was a sight to behold.'

'I wish it was still there, but it got destroyed in the 1860s. Such a shame.'

'Yes, it's not good when things like that happen.' Ned looked at the book and leaned towards the coffee table. He picked it up and flicked through it. 'It would have been nice if they'd managed to get some photos of the fountain, wouldn't it?'

'I suppose photography would have been something very new at that time.' Ailsa took another drink thoughtfully. 'So much is lost, isn't it? We're lucky now that we have camera-phones.'

'Yes. Unless you were good at art, you really lost all those little moments.'

'We kind of think they were just static pictures — all those old paintings and suchlike. It's hard to remember there were living, breathing people behind them.' Ailsa's thoughts wandered to Lady Eleanor, frozen in her wedding dress on the staircase. Not for the first time, she wished she could meet Ella

26

— but not in a ghost form. In a human form. Yes, a human Ella would be beyond exciting.

She was just about to voice that thought to Ned, when she realised his attention had been caught by something over her shoulder.

Ailsa followed his gaze and, when he spoke, he sounded astonished. 'Well now. Would you credit it. It's snowing.'

'Really?' Ailsa put her glass down and jumped to her feet. She ran over to the window. 'So it is! I wonder if it'll settle? It's usually too wet, this close to the coast.'

'I've seen some heavy snowfall over here before.'

Ailsa sensed he had moved close beside her and sure enough he leaned towards the window, looking outside. 'I don't know if it will settle, particularly. It's melting on the tarmac.'

'Probably just as well. We don't want guests snowed in. Or unable to get here. That's the worry.'

'I can think of worse places to be

trapped in a snowfall.' Ned smiled and turned his back to the window, leaning against the sill, folding his arms.

'Oh gosh, absolutely!' agreed Ailsa. 'It must have been beautiful when the Carricks lived here — not having to go anywhere, not worrying about getting to work. Just enjoying looking out at the weather and warming their toes by the fireplace.'

'Mulled wine and mince pies and music,' added Ned, nodding. 'I'm sure they had their little amusements outside too.'

'I'm sure they did. You know, I was chatting to Tara before and she was teasing me. She said she'd heard carols playing on the piano.' Ailsa laughed. 'I think she was trying to scare me. There's supposed to be a ghost in here who plays the piano, but I've never heard anything. Anyway, like I told her, Ella Carrick is only meant to play Mozart.'

'Ella,' said Ned, smiling. 'The girl in the Landseer.'

'Lady Eleanor, yes.'

'I doubt she would intentionally scare anybody,' said Ned. 'She seems far too nice for that.'

'I agree. I sometimes wonder what keeps her here, though. She must have loved the place very much, yet she was only a Carrick by marriage.'

'She grew up with the family though. She must have felt safe here — it was probably a big, scary world for her, without the love and support of her friends.' Ned was staring into the fireplace, deep in thought. 'I can't even begin to think about it — she was completely deaf by the time she was about seventeen, wasn't she? Maybe even earlier.' He shook his head. 'And to play the piano like she did — incredible.'

'Yes, it tells us quite a bit about her in the book. It really is a fascinating piece of work. It's advertised on our website as well, and we find a lot of people come here *because* they've read about the family.'

'That makes sense.' Ned turned and smiled at her. 'A fascinating family, I would say.'

'Completely. Yet I often wonder what their lives were actually *like*,' said Ailsa, almost without thinking. 'Whether anything could have been done to stop what happened. Whether anyone could have warned them. I sometimes wish I could go back in time, you know, just to advise them. It's silly, isn't it? We can't change the past. But I do so wish I could go back and meet Ella.'

'We can't change the past,' agreed Ned, 'but I think you have to understand that they lived in blissful ignorance.' He smiled wryly. 'They enjoyed the time they had.'

'Maybe that's the best way to be.' Ailsa smiled up at him. 'I *do* wish I could go back though, even just for a day, to see how they lived. It must have been wonderful at Christmas time. The Park is so special at any time of the year, but I think when we have the tree and the decorations up, it just raises it to that next level. Ah well, on that note, I should go. It's getting late, so much as I've loved chatting to you, I'd best get off to bed. Thank you for the mulled wine. It was very special to spend some time in here tonight, in the quiet. So lovely. But I've got a busy day tomorrow and two people who are relying on me to set them on the road to wedded bliss.' She looked around the drawing room. 'It'll look completely different tomorrow — full of flowers and people. But I quite like it as it is, to be honest. I'll just let the night porters work their magic in here and hide away.'

'And you say you'll be here overnight?'

'Yes. Like I said, my job is wonderful and sometimes I get to spend the night in a beautiful old house. I might bump into you tomorrow, but you'll have to forgive me if I don't chat much or if I rush by and look stressed. I've never done a Christmas Day wedding before, but it shouldn't be much different really.'

Ned smiled. 'I'm sure it'll be perfect.

And I'm sure I'll see you — I'll keep an eye out for you. Will you do the same for me?'

Ailsa laughed, secretly delighted that this dark-haired, dark-eyed man would be looking out for her. 'Of course I will. It was lovely meeting you. And thanks for your faith in me — what are the chances of me carrying off a Christmas Day wedding without going into melt-down? Don't answer that one!'

'I won't,' replied Ned, grinning. 'It was lovely to meet you too.'

She smiled and turned, collecting her iPad and hurrying out of the room before she was tempted to dilly-dally any longer. But how lovely; how lovely it had been to sit and chat with him, perfectly relaxed, in front of a low fire on Christmas Eve in Carrick Park. She wondered with a pang what her aunt and uncle were doing right now; given the time difference, they were probably waking up on Christmas morning. And they would be so much warmer over there than they would have been in

Derbyshire or the Borders with her other cousins.

Ailsa, personally, wouldn't have minded shivering with them all in Scotland like they usually did at Christmas. But if she couldn't spend Christmas Eve with her family, there were, she reasoned, worse places to be than Carrick Park. With Ned. In front of that fire.

She dipped her head and hid another smile. The encounter had made her feel a bit better about being alone at Christmas — despite the fact she'd be surrounded by about sixty people if you counted the wedding party. But that wasn't really the same, was it?

Ailsa passed Tara on reception as she headed up the stairs and waved at her. 'Happy Christmas!' Ailsa said, her voice sounding too loud in the quiet room. 'Not long now.'

'Just a couple of hours to go,' replied Tara, her hands wrapped around a mug of coffee. 'Then I'll be off. Hopefully the family trauma will be over by the time I get back. Mum always loses a

Christmas present at the last minute and Dad will still be wrapping his stuff. And my brothers will be drunk because they've been in the pub since tea-time.'

'Well have a lovely day anyway. I'll see you on the other side.'

'And I hope it goes well tomorrow! Have fun.'

'I'll try.' Ailsa cast a quick glance at the Landseer as she passed it, as she always did, and silently wished Ella a Merry Christmas, wherever she was tonight.

She climbed the extra set of steps that led up to the third floor and headed to one of the little rooms that were reserved for staff. The fact that they had been servants' quarters meant the rooms were small and functional, tucked away into the eaves, but were perfectly adequate. She let herself in, kicked her shoes off and put her iPad on the desk beneath the window.

Next stop was the bathroom, stripping her work clothes off as she went, and a quick shower before slipping into her pyjamas. It should have been too late to read. It should have been too late to do anything really, except sleep; but, once she had snuggled into the narrow bed, she reached out and grabbed the book she had left on the side table. It was her own copy of Becky Nelson's biography of the Carrick family. It was slightly tattered and she'd read it many times — but it was like an old friend. Something she could dip in and out of, especially just to settle her mind before bed. And that's what she intended to do tonight. Chatting to Ned had enthused her all over again about the Carrick Park she wished she could have known better.

Ella Carrick was the most fascinating part of that book — she, like Ailsa, had lost her parents when she was young and been brought up by an aunt. Unlike Ailsa, she had found a place where she belonged, unquestionably. That place, was in Adam Carrick's heart, and by the side of her best friend Lydia. Ailsa knew that the little girl

Ailsa had been would have fantasised over Ella's life and wished she could have lived it — despite the challenges it must have posed. Ella had managed and managed very well, it seemed. She never tired of reading about Ella and her fairy tale love story; it wasn't so pleasant reading about what had happened to her and Adam at the end, but the bits leading up to that, and how they eventually realised what they meant to each other, were beautiful.

On a night like tonight, when it was all magical and Christmassy and she was pleasantly tired, the idea of spending just one day with Ella, one Christmas Eve, perhaps, was almost a physical need. How wonderful it must have been! How wonderful to be in the midst of one's surrogate family and to love and be loved as Ella was.

It wasn't long before Ailsa found herself yawning and the written words before her beginning to blur together. She shifted position in bed, and her eyelids fluttered. They fluttered again, and, before she even realised it, she was fast asleep, the book discarded on the bed next to her,

It was the sound of the clock chiming twelve that woke her — but when she opened her eyes, she wasn't in her bed, and it clearly wasn't midnight that the clock was striking.

3

Christmas Past

1864

'What on earth . . . ?' whispered Ailsa. She was no longer in her bed, or even, it seemed, in her bedroom. Instead, she found herself standing almost exactly in the centre of another room — a drawing room, of all places. And she recognised it — oh yes, she recognised it, and she caught her breath as it struck her. This drawing room was definitely the drawing room of Carrick Park, but it certainly wasn't the drawing room she was accustomed to.

The furniture was all different, for a start; and there was a huge piano in front of the window with music neatly piled up on it — in a completely different place to where she was used to seeing the piano. A Christmas tree to rival the one by the staircase reached up almost to the ceiling — in fact, upon closer inspection, Ailsa noticed that it not only reached the ceiling, but the top six inches or so were bent over at a ninety-degree angle.

Ailsa tilted her head to the left, slightly dazed at the sight. The candles stuck haphazardly onto the branches glittered in the bright, wintry light that streamed through the windows.

'She has gone entirely overboard, hasn't she?' A man's voice in her ear startled her and she jumped. 'Oh, I'm so sorry — forgive me. I should have learned by now not to creep up on people.' He sounded amused, and Ailsa spun around to face a man in his late twenties. His fair hair, dark brown eyes and bright smile were familiar, and she stared at him, trying to think where she had seen him before.

'I can't imagine where she gets all these decorations,' the man continued. He waved his hands in the direction of the tree. 'All those little sugared fruits and gilded walnuts. Nobody even *likes* walnuts! And those horrid little dolls!' He walked over and tweaked a soft bodied, china-faced angel with silver wings from the tree. He stared at it for a moment or two and shook his head, before he tucked it back within the branches. Ailsa quite liked the angel — she didn't deserve to be called horrid at all. 'And of course, her German glass baubles. She always buys things from abroad that she thinks nobody else will have. Typical Lydia.'

'Lydia?' Ailsa found her voice and the man turned back to her.

'Well of course it's Lydia. I wouldn't buy them. Christmas is about the people you spend it with, not how many gewgaws you have on the tree. And the mere fact the damn tree is too damn tall for the room — she swears she measured it up. She swears she got Ella to help her. I really don't believe her.'

Ailsa blinked. 'Gewgaws'? And 'Lydia'? And 'Ella'? She noticed the man was wearing a waistcoat and tweedy-sort of trousers, and a white shirt with a wide lapel. 'Of course,' she said, faintly. 'Gewgaws.'

The man smiled and bowed slightly. 'Forgive me — I should probably introduce myself. I'm Adam Carrick. Lydia, the one responsible for these decorations is as you know, my sister. And you, I believe are Ailsa Cavendish?'

The fact that she was not Ailsa Cavendish, and was very much Ailsa McCormack, didn't register for a second as her host's name sunk in. 'Adam Carrick!'

Of course it was. *Of course* it was Adam Carrick. This man was the image of the small painting that had been hidden away for years in a dark corridor of the hotel. Becky Nelson, the author of the book Ailsa loved so much, had found a photograph of him, which had been taken around this time; thanks to that, Adam's likeness in this forgotten watercolour had been recognised.

'Yes — Adam Carrick — for my sins. I saw your husband earlier — I'm not sure where he went. I have no doubt that Lydia apprehended him and swept him away on a mission. I do apologise that I wasn't here to greet you both. Ned wasn't quite sure what time you would arrive.'

Ailsa just stared at Adam Carrick. 'Ned?' she finally managed.

'I know!' Adam laughed, his brown eyes crinkling up at the corners as he shook his head. 'He's never been the best time-keeper, has he? He admits that he was even late for your wedding. I apologise that we weren't there, although I know you wanted a quiet affair up in the Highlands. It would have helped, of course, had he *told* us you were getting married — but it was rather a whirlwind, wasn't it? Still, as he told me, once you know, you know. He said it was as if you'd known each other forever. Lydia found that desperately romantic.'

'Romantic,' repeated Ailsa, knowing she must sound like an idiot. 'Yes.' She cleared her throat. 'It *was* rather a whirlwind. It takes me by surprise even now, when I think about it.' It was nothing but the truth.

'Now, now!' A more familiar voice carried across the room as the door was flung open. 'Stop casting aspersions on my character!' And Ned Cavendish — looking very much at home here in Adam Carrick's drawing room — strode across the floor and caught Ailsa around the waist. He spun her around to face him and she stumbled, quickly realising she was encased in something that restricted her ribcage in a most uncomfortable manner and most definitely restricted her movement.

From her hips, she felt the swinging weight of a hooped skirt, wider at the back than it was at the front. For a moment, ridiculous as it seemed, Ailsa worried that she would be expected to sit down in this outfit, and had no idea how to accomplish it.

Ned leaned down as if he was going to kiss her. He was completely dressed for the part of Victorian country gentleman, as if he had just stepped out of the pages of a picture book, right down to the overcoat and cravat, a top hat tossed carelessly on to the chair as he walked in. He was, Ailsa realised with a little thrill, clean shaven which made his face even more sculptured and striking; but his hair was still as unruly as it had been in the Carrick Park she knew best. If this was a dream, good grief, he was welcome to be in it.

'How else could I get you here, decently, if not by pretending we were married?' he whispered, very close to her.

'Ned — ' she began in a low, shaky voice.

'Shhh,' he whispered. 'We're newly-weds.' And then he did kiss her, swiftly and firmly and as if he meant it. 'You wanted to see them. You wanted to see how they lived. Look — here's Ella. Tell me that she's not the most beguiling creature you've ever seen? Tell me you understand completely why Adam repaired that angel fountain for her?' He pulled away, but left his arm around her waist, turning her slightly so she was facing the door.

As if on cue, two bundles of energy burst into the room; two young women looking more like sisters than best friends, laughing at some shared joke. Both were tall and slim; both had golden, intricately styled hair. One of the girls had the most startlingly cornflower-blue eyes that Ailsa had ever seen, beyond the Landseer portrait on the Carrick Park staircase.

'Ella! Lydia! Please — our guests!' Adam Carrick had spoken, his voice warm and his gaze only for the girl with the blue eyes. 'We have just been admiring your Christmas tree. What went wrong?' He pointed to the tree-top, and two pairs of eyes followed his fingertip. One pair of eyes, the cornflower-blue ones, slid back to him, and focused firmly on his face. 'I think it's a little too tall,' Adam continued.

The girl with the blue eyes smiled, a little blush creeping across her cheeks, but she didn't speak.

'It was Ella's fault,' replied the girl with brown eyes, far too smartly. 'She misread the measurements.'

'Lydia, I don't think it was Ella's fault,' said Adam. 'Tell the truth.'

'Lydia!' The blue-eyed girl transferred her attention to the other girl. 'Did you blame me? You're the one who wrote the measurements down! I'm sure you didn't write exactly what I told you.'

'Oh, all right.' Lydia shrugged. 'I admit it, I added a tiny bit on to the measurements you gave me.' She demonstrated by holding her finger and thumb a small way apart. 'I thought the room was bigger than you said.'

'I tried to take into account that you would have to use a pot or a stand. So of course I told you it was smaller than it was. But you didn't believe me.' Ella — for this had to be her — looked at Ailsa and smiled shyly. 'I promise I am not as stupid as you may think. Despite the fact that she had me standing on a chair with a measuring tape in my hand for quite some time.'

'I never thought you were stupid,' said Ailsa, hardly believing that she was talking to Lady Eleanor Carrick. But of course, she wasn't Lady Eleanor Carrick, was she? She wasn't married to Adam. Ailsa had read the book dozens of times; she knew Ella's story. At this point in time, wherever she was in time, this girl was plain Ella Dunbar. She'd never had a Christmas as Lady Eleanor Carrick. She'd married in the September of 1865 and had died in November of that year. So this had to be before that — Ailsa took a wild guess at 1864. Perhaps. It would do for now, anyway.

Ella's eyes widened a little, then she smiled. 'Thank you,' she said, simply.

'Oh!' Lydia interrupted, putting her hand on Ella's arm to get her attention. 'We haven't even introduced ourselves, have we?' She curtsied, very prettily, to Ailsa. 'I'm Lydia, Adam's sister. This is my dearest friend in all the world, Eleanor Dunbar. But we all call her

Ella. You, well, you simply *must* be Ailsa, Ned's wife. I'm so sorry it's taken so long to meet you — we kept asking and asking Ned, all through the summer, and he promised he'd bring you to see us. And then he had the audacity to marry you, all in secret, before we could do that — and now!' She flung her arms wide, a smile on her face. 'Now, we finally have the chance. Thank you for coming to us for Christmas. Ned *always* comes and we couldn't have done it without him. We are so utterly pleased to have you. I did ask our cousin Jacob as well, but he can't come. He has commitments elsewhere apparently. So you, darling Ailsa, will have *all* our attention and we'll soon have you as much a part of our family as Ned here.'

'Thank you,' replied Ailsa, not really sure what else she could say. She knew nothing about why she was apparently in Carrick Park, sometime circa 1864. She was pretty certain she was dreaming and she'd wake up in the morning

— Christmas morning — in her narrow little bed in the staff quarters of the hotel and find out she'd returned to real life and she had a wedding to supervise. However, despite the strangeness of the situation, she found herself relieved that she wouldn't have to face Cousin Jacob — if ever something was destined to make the situation even more uncomfortable and more weird, it would be sharing a turkey with the man who still had such a dark reputation, over one hundred and fifty years after he'd lived. She wasn't a good actress and she couldn't pretend she knew absolutely nothing. She couldn't —

'I'll help you,' murmured Ned, as if he'd read her mind. 'Just go with it for now.' In a louder voice, he responded to Lydia's speech. 'Thank you, Lydia. As always, you are a wonderful hostess, and I'm enchanted to be here.'

He swept a low, courtly bow to Lydia and she put her hands over her mouth and giggled. 'Oh Ned! Stop it,' she demanded. 'But honestly — what do you think of my tree?'

'Your tree?' asked Ned. 'Well, my darling, I think it's very — you. It's the biggest one yet, I think.'

'Ned Cavendish!' she shrieked. 'You horror!'

Lydia looked so shocked, that Ailsa couldn't help smiling. She was exactly how Ailsa had always imagined Lydia to be. Ailsa cast a glance over to Ella. Ella was looking at Lydia, her eyes travelling between her friend and Ned as she followed the conversation. And Adam, God bless him, had eyes only for Ella Dunbar.

'Oh — has anyone shown you to your rooms yet?' asked Lydia, suddenly addressing Ailsa. 'We've been busy with the decorations, so I'm afraid I don't know myself what is happening.'

'No.' Ailsa shook her head. 'I'm afraid I don't know where I'm sleeping at all.' That, again, was the truth.

Ned took Ailsa's hand and smiled at Lydia. 'My wife and I haven't been here very long ourselves, so we're not at all worried that we haven't been shown to our rooms yet. All in good time.'

'Absolutely,' replied Lydia. 'Allow me to rectify it, though. Please — take a seat and I'll ring for someone.'

She indicated a couch and Ailsa hesitated for a moment — she was going to have to sit, wasn't she? She just hoped that she could manage by perching on the edge of the thing. She had an image of the brides she had met over the years who had insisted on full-skirted creations, and recalled that, after seeing their struggles, she had promised herself that, should she ever get married, she would go for something straighter. Asking for help to go to the loo wasn't something she ever wanted to do on her own wedding day, and goodness knows she'd had to do her fair share of bridesmaid herding and toilet door guarding so the girls could answer the call of nature.

Ailsa walked slowly over to the seat and sat carefully on the edge as she had anticipated. She hoped she'd managed it elegantly enough and flashed a look at Ned, who quickly looked away, trying to hide a smile.

Lydia hurried over to the bell-pull and Ella stood awkwardly in the middle of the room, following her friend's movements, until Adam appeared and took her by the arm.

'Come along,' he said. 'I think I know where you'd prefer to sit.'

He began to lead her to the piano and Ella resisted him, casting a worried look at Ailsa. 'Oh no. I'm sure Ailsa doesn't want to hear me play anything.'

'I'm sure she does,' said Adam. 'It's Christmas Eve and we always have music from you on Christmas Eve. Bach's *Christmas Oratorio*, or some carols — '

'Carols?' Ailsa couldn't help herself. 'I thought you played Mozart!' Adam stopped and turned, forcing Ella to turn with him so they were both looking at Ailsa. Ailsa's cheeks burned as she realised she'd been talking to the girl's back — very impolite in any situation, but especially in this one.

Adam, however, smiled encouragingly and continued the conversation smoothly. 'Oh, we do enjoy Mozart at Carrick Park, don't we Ella? I swear, it's difficult to get her to play anything else.'

'Almost impossible,' chimed in Lydia, who had appeared at Ailsa's side again. She threw herself onto the sofa next to her and made an altogether better job of it than Ailsa had done in her flouncy frock. 'Ella is so absolutely stubborn, we can't change her mind at all.'

'That's not true!' replied Ella with a laugh. 'I just prefer Mozart, that's all.' She looked at Ailsa and smiled shyly. 'If you want me to, I'll play Mozart. If you don't, I'll play something for Christmas. Or I needn't play at *all*. I would hate you to feel as if you had to be polite and listen to me. I'm rather terrible anyway.'

She tried to tug her arm away from Adam, who pulled her even closer and shook his head. 'You're a liar,' he said. 'You're the best musician I've ever come across.'

The love was shining from his eyes and Ailsa bit her lip.

She could weep for this pair, she really could, dreaming or not. 'Some carols would be lovely,' she managed, and smiled at Ella.

Ella blushed and looked at her feet, then back up at Ailsa. 'All right. But only one or two — I get more and more rusty every year with them. I forget — ' She cut herself off and smiled, then nodded. 'All right.' She disconnected herself from Adam and turned decisively, picking up her skirts and hurrying over to the piano. Ailsa knew she had been going to say something along the lines of how she forgot what the carols sounded like and she felt dreadful for her.

'Well I must say, it'll be nice to have a change,' said Lydia. 'Did Mozart *do* anything for Christmas? Now *that* would be interesting to find out.' She tapped her fingers against her chin thoughtfully, clearly not expecting an answer.

Ailsa felt Ned's hand on her shoulder and he squeezed it reassuringly. 'You're doing well,' he whispered as he stood behind her.

She turned and looked up at him. 'I can't do this!' she muttered. 'What if I trip myself up? I've seen enough. They're obviously very happy. Can we go back now?'

Ned shook his head. 'No. But just listen — isn't that wonderful?'

The first few notes of *Silent Night* were tentatively breaking the silence as Ella found her way around the melody for the first time in a year. She frowned and seemed to be concentrating on the piano, then all of sudden the simple tune soared and took flight, and Ailsa was entranced. The music gave way to a version of *It Came Upon a Midnight Clear*, and finally died off into the richness of *O Holy Night*. Ailsa hardly dared to breathe. She knew those notes would haunt her forever.

Ella laid her hands on the keys, her cheeks even more pink as the recital ended. She glanced up at Adam who had, at some point, taken to leaning on the piano, as close to his angel as he could possibly get, and then her blue eyes swept across the audience and settled on Ailsa.

'Was that all right?' she asked. 'It's so long since I played those, I never know if I'm still doing them correctly.'

'You are astounding,' said Ailsa, staring at her in awe. 'I've never heard those songs played so beautifully.'

'Oh! Thank you.' Ella smiled, genuinely astonished at the praise.

'And considering Ella hasn't *heard* them for so long, we must applaud her.' Lydia, jumped to her feet whilst clapping, quite unabashed at the words she had just spoken.

Ailsa gawped at her, wondering at the audacity of her hostess, embarrassed on Ella's behalf, but then she heard a laugh and looked across to see Ella shaking her head prettily.

Ella threw her arms out to the side and grinned at Ailsa. 'It's very true. You never know what you'll end up with at Christmas. Which is why I prefer my Mozart. I know where I am with him.'

'And whilst we were otherwise engaged, your luggage has been taken to your rooms, hopefully it's been unpacked and I'll show you where you're to sleep tonight,' chipped in Lydia. 'Come along.' She held out her hand to Ailsa.

Ailsa reached out, half-wondering if she would be able to touch Lydia — after all, surely, if this *wasn't* a dream, she was just a shadow, a rip in the veil. None of this was real and she wasn't really here, was she?

As her hand connected with Lydia's and she realised how warm and firm her hostess' grip was, she thought she might have to re-evaluate that one as well.

'There should be some clothing laid out for you already,' said Lydia. 'I gave the maids some instructions and, I'm happy to see, that the weather has obliged us this year. Last year, it was terrible. Can you recall, Ned? It was so dreary and wet, we were quite trapped indoors.'

Ailsa looked at Ned, who, by rights, should have been somewhere in the twenty-first century last year, perhaps celebrating Gabe's birthday with him and not at Carrick Park.

'It was awful, wasn't it?' agreed Ned. 'It just never stopped raining!'

'Quite grim,' replied Lydia nodding. 'Look! Look Ailsa — see what good luck you've brought us this year.' She stopped in the hallway and hurried over to the door. 'This is my absolute favourite view, and you won't have seen it from within the house. It's far more picturesque when viewed from the warmth inside the Park. See?' Lydia flung the door open and Ailsa gasped. Outside, was a patchwork of white. Snow decorated the branches of the trees, and the carriage-drive — which Ailsa knew better as the main drive up to the hotel — was rutted, the frost and snow topping each rut like icing sugar.

As far as she could see, the gardens stretched out, pristine white, shining like silver, untouched and begging to be walked in. Ailsa reckoned there was a good six inches of snow.

'It's beautiful!' she cried. 'I was just saying to Ned before we got here — '

She stopped herself, but Lydia looked at her questioningly. 'What were you saying to him?'

Ailsa flushed. 'I was saying to him that I wondered what it was like here with all the snow,' she finished, unsure of whether she had or had not been saying that to him.

'And now you know,' replied Lydia, triumphantly. 'And I'm so pleased, as it makes our activities much more exciting. Come along, let's get you to your room and we can play in the snow after that.'

She closed the door, and took Ailsa's arm again, walking up the stairs with her, chattering to her about inconsequential items, asking her to admire the holly and the ivy that she and Ella had wound around the banisters and the family portraits. Ailsa halted at the fork in the stairs, thrown by the fact there was no Landseer there. For as long as she had worked at Carrick Park, Ella's picture had graced the wall, apart from when it had enjoyed its brief sojourn at the British Museum. The Landseer itself had been returned to Carrick Park as part of Lydia's legacy. It had moved out of the Park with her when she had sold the place, then came back after her own death, many years later.

Lydia halted with her, following her gaze towards the huge, blank wall. 'Oh, I know. It's a terribly dreary space, isn't it? That's why I hung that little portrait of Adam there. It needed cheering up. It really needs a lovely *big* portrait there. One day.' She smiled at the watercolour of her brother and Ailsa felt little prickles along the back of her neck. This was the picture at Carrick Park that now hung alongside the Landseer; someone had decided to put Ella and Adam side by side after reading the book about them. It was beyond weird to see it here, exactly as it had been once upon a time. Ailsa leaned towards it, astonished at how fresh the colours looked — to be fair, it hadn't faded too much over the years anyway.

'It's a good likeness,' she told Lydia, who blushed and smiled.

'Thank you, I think so,' she replied. 'Your room is just along here. It's not too far from Ella's. She's always had the same one, ever since she was little. We've practically grown up together, Ned might have told you?'

'I'd heard that was the case,' said Ailsa carefully. There was no need to let Lydia know she had gleaned that information from a book published so many years after they had all lived. 'Ella seems lovely.'

'Oh she is. And she won't like me for this, but I have something planned which may amuse us later.' Lydia stopped outside a door. 'It's this one. Ned likes the view out to sea. I don't know why. He just says he likes to travel. I don't even know where he disappears to, he never tells us. But I'm sure you know where he goes.' Lydia smiled and pushed open the door. 'He's always back for Christmas though. Says he'd never miss a Christmas at Carrick Park.'

'Oh.' Ailsa felt a little faint. 'Yes. So he tells me. Thank you, Lydia. You're very kind.' She looked in at the room. A fire was crackling merrily in the grate and someone had even decorated the mantelpiece with a festive garland to welcome them. A bowl of holly, pine cones and crystallised slices of orange graced the windowsill. The odd cinnamon stick poked out of the display and the room smelled delightfully of an old-fashioned Christmas.

'I'll leave you to get ready,' said Lydia with a mischievous twinkle in her eye. 'I hope you don't hate me for it.'

★   ★   ★

The thing that, potentially, might have made Ailsa hate Lydia, was an ice-skating outfit, complete with skates. Looking at the red and white checked skirt and jacket wasn't too scary; but the ice-skates were a different matter.

'Ah, it didn't take her long to organise today's excursion.' Ned popped his head in at the bedroom door. 'May I come in?'

'Of course.' Ailsa gestured around her. 'Apparently, it's your room anyway.'

'It is.' Ned went over to the window and peered out. 'It's got one of the best views in the whole house.'

'I can't skate,' Ailsa said, flatly. 'I've been twice and was useless both times.'

'I've done it quite a bit more than that and I'm still useless,' replied Ned. 'I'm not sure where she's intending to go skating.'

'The lake in the grounds?' asked Ailsa.

Ned shook his head. 'No, Adam said he went down there earlier and the ice looks too thin. I can only think of the pond outside of the Abbey. It's a bit higher up there and it'll be an excuse to get the sleigh out.'

'A *sleigh*?' Ailsa stared at Ned. 'What on earth are they doing with a sleigh? And surely we can't get in the Abbey grounds to skate, I mean there's bound to be security.'

'It's 1864,' said Ned with a grin. 'What security would there be? And of course they've got a sleigh. This is Lydia Carrick we're talking about here — all the most up to date fads and fancies find their way to Carrick Park. Anyway, having a sleigh was quite common. It was the best way to travel over the snow, if you think about it. Lydia has a four-seater one. Which means Adam will be driving, no doubt.'

Ailsa sat down on the high bed with a very realistic *flumph* of petticoats and skirts. 'It's actually 1864? I still think this is a dream — it has to be.' She looked up at Ned. 'It *is* a dream, isn't it? One of those lucid ones where you can all interact and you know you're dreaming, but you enjoy it so don't let yourself wake up.' She pointed at him. 'You've been in my dreams before — that's how I know. That's why I'm comfortable with you here. That's why I'm okay being Ailsa Cavendish. Because I *know* you. We aren't here. We can't be. Good God. It's like being in a living Christmas card.'

'I've been in dreams before? That's interesting. But a word of advice — don't mention Christmas cards. They weren't really massively popular in 1864, and the ones that were exchanged certainly wouldn't have the sort of pictures on *you* would recognise as a Christmas design.'

Ailsa shook her head. 'I won't. Thanks. But how the heck am I supposed to get this outfit off and that one on?' She plucked at her skirts. Again, they felt pretty real, fabric-wise.

'They have maids for that sort of thing. Unless you want me to — ' Ned's eyes twinkled.

'No! Good grief, no. No way are you seeing me in my corsets.'

'All right. I'll make myself scarce. Ring that bell over there and I'm sure someone will come up.' He nodded towards a button on the wall and Ailsa knew that too would be connected to the bells that lined the corridor in the staff area of the hotel. She'd often looked at them and wondered what it would have been like when they rang and the servants dashed out to see what was required — she'd thought it again earlier today, or last night, or whenever it was that she had been leaving the office in her own time and place. Well, now she was going to find out what it was like to use the bell from a guest's point of view.

'Okay. I'll see you later then.' She glanced at Ned, who was looking very dapper in his overcoat and was clutching a warmer looking hat. 'You're ready?'

'I am. I'll see you downstairs. I just need my skates.' He came around to the side of the bed and picked up a pair of ice skates. 'These ones are mine. See the scuff mark on that toe? I managed to plough into a rock a few years ago. Almost broke my nose as I fell.' He laughed and raised the skates up in a kind of salute. 'See you soon. Oh — and another little hint. Don't say 'okay' to these guys, okay?' His eyes twinkled. 'It wasn't in use until World War Two and I believe it was an Americanism.'

'Oh.' Ailsa hadn't known that.'

'Oh indeed. I'll see you later — *okay*?' He winked at her. 'And the only thing I *must* insist on, now I've got you on your own, is that you never, *ever* try to meddle and tell Ella or Adam things that they don't need to know. Okay?' His eyes hardened and Ailsa blushed.

Ailsa nodded. 'Okay — I mean, of course.' Her cheeks burned as she watched him leave the room, swinging the skates as he went. She stood up and walked over to the button. She stared at it for a moment, and eventually pushed it; then she sat back down and waited.

Sure enough, a maid came scurrying in, and helped Ailsa undress and redress as efficiently as possible. She shivered a little in the cotton undergarments, but couldn't resist taking a peek to see what she looked like with her figure forced into a corset.

Never a particularly stick-thin person anyway, Ailsa already had natural curves and went in and out where she should. In this Victorian torture garment they called a corset, though, she guessed she could rival any glamour model with her boobs pushed up so high and so proudly, and her stomach and waist sucked in until she could, almost, encircle it with her hands.

As she stared at herself over the white-capped head of the maid who was fussing with the skirts, Ailsa felt sorry for those poor Victorian women who had been forced into maternity corsets. If it squashed *her* to this extent, she could only imagine what it must have done to the poor baby. If she'd been pregnant in this era, she would have refused, point blank to wear one. Having said that, that idea came with the wisdom of her own time. She shuddered, hoping she would have taken a sensible approach, regardless. She put the idea out of her head and instead turned her attention back to her skating outfit.

It was a pretty, if functional, set of a skirt and jacket, with a little black hat she could perch on her head. The skirt was slightly shorter than the one she had been wearing when she arrived here, and she was smoothing it down, when the maid stood up and went to pick up a pair of tall, button-up boots in the corner of the room.

The girl produced a button hook and smiled at Ailsa. 'I'll be as quick as I can, Mrs Cavendish,' she said. 'Please, take a seat.'

It seemed to take an inordinately long time for the maid to do the boots up, but Ailsa couldn't help but be fascinated by the whole process. Her own fingers would have fumbled sausage-like at the delicate pearl buttons, and it was with a genuine sense of gratitude that she thanked the girl at the end of the task.

'Thank you . . . I'm sorry. I don't know your name.'

The maid blushed and curtsied. 'It's Elizabeth, Mrs Cavendish. And it's a pleasure to help you.'

'I'm very grateful,' said Ailsa sincerely.

The girl curtsied again. 'I'm going to go and see if Miss Ella needs me now.'

'I'm sure she'll appreciate that,' replied Ailsa. The maid nodded and smiled, and hurried out of the room, closing the door softly behind her.

The only thing now, was for Ailsa to pick up the skates and try to see how they would strap onto the boots. It looked straightforward enough, and she was sure someone would help her at the other end, so she took a deep breath and made her own way out of the door.

She didn't need telling how to get along the corridors and back to the staircase. She had worked at Carrick Park long enough, and began to walk quickly through the house. Then she made a conscious effort to slow down. This is what it was like when the Park was a home. She needed to see it as it was and look at the paintings on the walls, the furniture in the alcoves, the cabinets full of china and ornaments and the bowls of flowers and greenery on the tables. Every so often, there was a festive decoration — a swathe of fir, or a branch of holly. Another bowl of pine cones and crystallised orange. It was exactly as she had imagined a Christmas at Carrick Park would look like.

She descended the staircase, feeling every inch a grand lady and saw Ned at the bottom, talking to Adam. He turned when she walked down and smiled, then held his hand out for her to clasp, just as if he'd never said anything about her meddling in Ella and Adam's relationship. She could tell that, as far as he was concerned, he'd told her and that was it — no need to hold a grudge of any description. Which was good.

'You look ready for some fun,' Ned said warmly and squeezed her hand. 'Don't worry, I've told Adam that you're not very good at skating, just like me.'

'To be perfectly honest,' said Adam, 'Lydia is the best one out of the three of us. I think that's why she wants to do this. She's a terrible show off.'

'What's that about me?' Lydia breezed in looking delightful in a deep blue velvet skating outfit, pulling some white kid gloves onto her hands.

'I'm just telling them how much of a show off you are,' said Adam.

'Oh, I know that already,' said Ned with a laugh and Lydia poked him in the arm.

'How dare you!' she said, but she was laughing as she spoke. 'The sleigh is almost ready. It's being brought around to the front very soon. I suppose Ella is still getting ready?'

'Elizabeth went to her after me,'

offered Ailsa. 'She shouldn't be long.'

'Excellent.' Lydia looked at the door. 'We'll wait for her here, but as it's Ailsa's first Christmas with us, perhaps you would like to go and see the sleigh being brought around? It's a wonderful sight — I never tire of it. But as a guest, I think you'll enjoy it more.' Lydia smiled in that confident sort of way she did, which meant, Ailsa now realised, that she had done something she deemed praiseworthy.

'Thank you. Yes, that would be lovely,' agreed Ailsa.

'Come on then.' That was Ned as he transferred her hand into the crook of his arm. He'd been holding her hand the whole time and she had enjoyed that feeling of security. She cast a look up at her supposed-husband and caught his profile as he looked towards the door himself. He really was a very good-looking man. His hair was obviously meant to be tamed in some sensible 1864 hairstyle, but it wasn't. It just looked ruffled and slightly messy and very, very attractive.

A butler appeared out of the shadows and bowed as he opened the main doors. Despite Lydia showing her the outdoors earlier, Ailsa still expected to see the vista she was used to — the tarmac road leading up to the hotel. Maybe one or two cars in the disabled spaces right outside, the neat gardens and the lamps either side of the drive to guide cars in when it was dark.

Of course, there was a fresh, white driveway, and she was delighted to hear the faint jingle of bells and the muffled thudding of hooves in the snow, followed by a whinny as a horse appeared, pulling a sleigh behind it, shaking its chestnut mane proudly and huffing steam out through its nostrils. She did not expect, however, to see the sleigh decorated with more greenery and more holly and tartan ribbons with a pile of tartan blankets and cushions on the seats and a sturdy box secured on the back of it.

'It's beautiful!' she whispered stunned. 'Oh Ned, isn't it *beautiful*?'

'It is. As she said, it's always a sight to behold. But she put the tartan in it this year to honour your heritage, my love.'

'Lydia!' Ailsa spun around, her skirts swishing pleasingly around her calves, to thank her hostess for the opportunity to see the sleigh in all its glory; but her attention was arrested by Ella coming down the stairs, dressed in a gorgeous, emerald-green skating dress, trimmed with white fur. On her head, was a little white fur hat and around her neck, hung on a black string, was a white fur muff. Her skates were dangling from one hand as she made her way carefully down the stairs, holding onto the banister, little honey-coloured curls bouncing around her cheeks.

Had it not been for the fact that the Landseer depicted Ella in a white, swansdown-trimmed dress, then she might quite easily have stepped out of her portrait and onto the landing. The likeness, Ailsa noted incredulously, was splendid.

'I'm so sorry,' Ella said as she

stepped off the bottom stair. 'I couldn't find my hat, but now I have it.' She tapped her head as if to prove her point and smiled. 'Are we all ready? Is everyone waiting for me?'

'Yes, we're just about to go,' said Lydia. She hooked her arm into her friend's and led her out of the hallway. 'I've had the sleigh decorated with the bells again. It looks wonderful.'

Lydia paused on the top step outside and dragged Ella back around to face everyone. 'Adam — you're driving, of course. Ella and Ailsa can sit together facing the direction of travel, and I will sit next to Ned, and we two shall look at where we've been. We've seen the scenery dozens of times, haven't we Ned? I know Ailsa will want to see where we are heading and I know that Ella just feels happier when she can look ahead as well.'

'It saves any nasty surprises,' Ella explained to Ailsa. 'If I know there's a rut coming, I don't jump so much when we hit it.'

'That makes perfect sense,' replied Ailsa with a nod. It was odd what you perhaps had to consider when you'd lost your hearing. She wondered if the reason Ella had come so carefully down the stairs was something to do with her balance. The inner ear controlled all of that, of course. So maybe it was. Or, Ailsa thought, amused, it was because, like any young girl who knew she looked absolutely stunning, Ella just wanted to make an entrance.

'Shall we?' asked Ned, gesturing to the sleigh. It was his turn to lead Ailsa down the steps and to the side of the sleigh. He helped her up and she sat down, feeling the thing shift a little with her weight. Next up was Ella, then Lydia, then finally Ned. Adam thanked the driver, and swapped places with him; then he cracked the whip and with a shuffle and a lurch, they were off.

'Have a blanket.' Ella handed one to Ailsa. 'It can get chilly. It's best to be all wrapped up on the way. And then it's double blankets on the way back, when everybody is grumpy and cold.'

Ailsa took the blanket, still not quite believing that she was sitting next to the future Lady Eleanor Carrick, who was as solid as Ailsa was in the twenty-first century.

'Lydia, darling, is there any reason why you didn't ask Blackie to pull the sleigh?' asked Ella, quite icily, once she had made sure Ailsa was sufficiently bundled up in tartan wool.

'Because, my dear, he is simply far too fat and he would sink into the snow,' said Lydia.

Ella pulled a face. 'I have to agree,' she said. She looked at Ailsa. 'Blackie is my little horse. He is absolutely as fat as butter and would hate to come out of his nice warm stall and do something like this. Do you know, they even light fires in those stables to keep the animals warm! Blackie is incredibly spoiled. Everyone loves him and they all give him far too many treats.'

Lydia leaned forward so she was in Ella's line of vision. 'Ella doesn't exercise him enough, that's the truth of the matter.'

'The truth of the matter is that I'm a dreadful horsewoman and nobody will come with me! And it's dull on my own, anyway.'

'Nobody comes with you because of the fact you *are* a dreadful horse-woman!' said Lydia indignantly.

Ella laughed and leaned forward, weighing a little bunch of silver bells in her hand. Ailsa noticed how she barely held them, letting them vibrate on her palm instead.

'I always loved sleigh bells,' Ella said, to nobody in particular, 'and Blackie would look a *dear* wearing them in his bridle.'

Ailsa felt uncomfortable in a way she had no words to describe. Ella had been out with Blackie when she died, or so the story went. And here she was, admitting that she wasn't the best of horsewomen. Surely she could maybe just advise Ella to try and ride a little more, so that she could control the horse if need be . . .

Ailsa cast a glance at Ned, who just fixed his eyes on her, a warning in the almost-black depths. His voice came back to her: *the only thing I must insist on is that you never, ever try to meddle and tell Ella or Adam things that they don't need to know.* But why in heaven's name should she abide by that? She had a clear chance to help her and —

But Lydia, her eyes sharp and her mind even sharper, saw the look that passed between them; of course she could only guess at the reason why.

So Lydia apparently made her best guess and, before Ailsa could pursue the matter, muttered into her blanket, taking care that Ella couldn't read her: 'She always *did* love sleigh bells, but I can't honestly say how long it's been since she heard the damn things.' She frowned, and glared at the passing scenery, as if it was the moors' fault that her best friend had gradually gone deaf. 'I would suggest it's been four or five years. Certainly, there was nothing there by the time we had our Season and we were seventeen then. Gosh, a whole three years ago! Yes, she just told me that she woke up one day and sort of realised the sounds had finally disappeared — she'd said she came to understand, later, that she'd almost given up on *listening* by that point. It was too difficult. She was reading lips to understand us, re-learning her dratted piano, somehow, before she forgot — '

Lydia scowled some more and Ailsa wondered if she had taken it just as badly as Ella. Certainly, Lydia liked to be in control, and if she couldn't do anything for her friend, she would have felt dreadful. 'And she said she'd tried to listen to the flames crackling in the grate and she couldn't hear them, then she tried to hear the bells in the servants' corridor — she just stood in front of them and waited until someone rang one and she saw it jump around but that was it. And then of course she was out by that silly old angel fountain in the courtyard, breaking her heart and getting so very, very angry over the whole thing; and Adam found her. And she couldn't hear him, and he's got the loudest voice of *any* of us.' Finally, coming to the end of her rant, Lydia pressed her lips together and pulled a blanket further around herself. 'So now you know as much as I know. Which is why I always go overboard with bloody bells on this damn sleigh.'

'I don't suppose that's any reason to use such terrible language, Lydia Carrick,' scolded Ned good-humouredly, but she just shrugged into the blankets some more and tucked her chin into her chest.

'Do you think the ice will be safe enough to skate on?' Ella sat back, releasing the sleigh bells and looked questioningly at Ned. *Of course!* Ailsa realised Ella wouldn't have had a clue what they were saying if her attention was on the little bells, and the change of subject threw her a little.

'I should think so,' replied Ned smoothly, as if Lydia hadn't spent the last few minutes talking about her fellow passenger. 'And then Lydia will be able to show off until her heart is content.'

'I hope I don't fall again,' moaned Ella, huddling up under the blanket much as Lydia was doing. 'It's not very pleasant.'

Adam risked looking around at them, as he reached a straight bit of track, the moors spreading out either side of them, white as far as the eye could see, the sea a pale grey-ish ribbon on the right.

'I heard someone mention ice. And then worry about falling down — Miss Dunbar, eh? It's not far now, and we'll find out if it's decent to skate on and whether we can all stay upright. Can you see it, ladies?' He pointed with the whip to the Abbey, and the sight of that familiar building in the distance made Ailsa's stomach contract. The hulking ruin looked very much as it did in modern times — but she knew in this waking dream that there'd be no car park nearby, and no sign of any public access at all.

'We can see it!' cried Lydia, suddenly brightening and almost falling out of the sleigh as she twisted around and half hung out of the thing.

Ella grabbed her around the waist and pulled her back down to her seat. 'And we'll *never* get there if you end up on the ground, in a snowdrift, because you can't sit still!'

Adam laughed and cracked the whip again. The horse found a burst of speed and trotted along the lane.

'Almost there,' he shouted over his shoulder. 'Hang on to your hats, ladies.'

4

1864

Ned cast a glance at Ailsa. She still looked stunned, but damn she wore that skating outfit well. There were roses in her creamy cheeks and her eyes were the colour of polished mahogany, glittering in the frosty light, wide with surprise as if she was trying to take everything in and remember it forever — which, to be fair, she probably was doing.

He would have enjoyed staying in the room with her while she got changed, but maybe that was something he would have to reserve for another time, God willing.

Unable to help himself, wanting to touch her again, he reached over and tucked a stray lock of hair under her hat. 'That's better,' he said, smiling at her. She reached up and touched the hat, as if she was trying to make sure that was real as well. 'I don't suppose you've ever seen the Abbey like this before?' he asked, his lips curving into a smile, knowing full well what the answer would be.

'Never,' she replied. 'I can honestly say I've never seen the Abbey from this angle before.' Her eyes slid over his shoulder and her chin tilted and he knew she was looking at the grey stones, trying to superimpose the twenty-first century images of the Abbey onto the open fields and narrow, snow-filled tracks she was surrounded by.

'It's quite impressive, isn't it?' he asked.

'Very.' She cleared her throat and asked a question. 'Can you get into St Mary's church from this direction?'

'You can,' Ned replied. 'It's a lovely church.'

'Ideal for a wedding,' she said, fixing him with a look that spoke volumes.

Ned sat back and folded his arms. He

shook his head, ever so slightly, so she knew that he knew she was trying to press certain issues. They'd had that conversation. That church was, of course, where Ella and Adam had been married — or, more correctly, where they *would* be married next year.

Ned knew Ailsa was full of good intentions; he knew that she wanted to help — but there was too much she didn't understand about his life. It wasn't her fault. She'd been thrown into the middle of this Christmas on the wings of a wish. That was the hardest thing about her being here — the fact that, as she always did, she wanted to dive in and help people on the road to their starry-bright future. He wasn't surprised that she was in the job she was — helping love-struck couples plan their perfect day. The fact that he and Ailsa had to pretend to be newlyweds, though, and be head over heels in love, was second nature to him. He'd done that before. He liked that part of being here with her very much.

Ailsa, however, still tried to plough ahead. 'Ella, if you were ever to marry, do you think you would marry here or at Yo — your *other* home?' Ned ducked his head and hid a smile. York. She'd almost said York — which was where Ella's family home was. But Ailsa, of course, wasn't supposed to know that, was she?

'Nice,' murmured Ned, his head still down and his arms folded. 'But be careful. I'll just stop you and you might not appreciate how I do it.' He raised his eyes and saw Ailsa's cheeks burn a little brighter as she pretended she hadn't heard him.

'Marry? Me?' Ella looked at Ailsa, quizzically. 'I don't think that will ever happen. I'm usually with Lydia, and she's always so much more talkative than I am. People love Lydia. I just wilt into the corner and smile a lot.' As if to prove her point, she smiled widely, right at Ailsa.

Ned found himself mesmerised by that smile. Ella really was a stunning young woman. Ned knew many men had fallen for her — himself included, in some small way, although he knew it was never meant to be. People just couldn't resist her.

Lydia, lost in a daydream, perked up at the mention of her name. 'Wilting into a corner?' She stared at her friend as if she couldn't quite comprehend what she had said. 'You never wilt. Stop pretending you do.'

'I do wilt. I always wilt next to you. You *make* a person wilt.'

'Rubbish! Utter tosh!' cried Lydia. She pulled her hand out of her muff and wagged a finger at Ella. 'You talk a lot of rubbish. I'm saying that very slowly, so you understand.'

'It's better for me if you just speak normally,' retorted Ella. 'Then you don't look so . . . odd.'

Ned smiled into his scarf. He hardly dared look at Ailsa. She would be horrified to think that the two young women she had expected to be paragons of virtue and sensibleness were just like any other hugely close, almost-sisters. They knew exactly what they wanted to say and said it. They never got upset with one another, never took offence and would side with each other until the day they died, should anyone argue back.

'They're always like this,' Ned told Ailsa. He didn't bother speaking into his scarf any more. The girls were entirely unaware of his conversation, sparking tartly off one another, as they always had done.

'I am baffled,' said Ailsa, shaking her head and looking at him. 'They're just — *normal.*'

'Well of course they are,' said Ned. 'What did you expect?'

'Victorian restraint, I think.'

'Well you won't get much of that with these two.' He grinned. 'Trust me. I've seen all this before, a hundred times over. And please — remember what I told you. It's important.'

'Well it's not my fault. It's all new to me!' said Ailsa. 'I'm not used to *this* sort of dream.'

Ned laughed; her disbelieving face

was an absolute picture.

And he loved her for it.

★ ★ ★

They soon made it to the Abbey with nobody tumbling out of the sleigh, their arguments forgotten and everybody intact.

'Will the horse be all right?' Ailsa asked anxiously as Ned helped her out. 'I don't like to think of him standing in the snow.'

'He'll be fine. He's got his own blanket on, as well as some extra ones; he'll be in the shelter of the walls and we'll build a little fire to keep him warm. There are some dry sticks and things on the back of the sleigh. They've done all this before. Look — Adam's making a start.'

Sure enough, Ailsa looked across and Adam was arranging some wood, murmuring to the horse who stood quietly as Lydia and Ella began unstrapping the harness between them.

'I had no idea they would know how to do that — let alone that they *would* do it,' said Ailsa in surprise. It was an altogether less privileged side to them than she had expected to see.

'They're quite nice people!' replied Ned with a laugh, 'And they've always spoiled their horses. You heard them talking about Blackie.'

'Yes about that. What harm would it do if I'd told her to just ride a bit more and get her confidence up?'

Ned didn't answer for a moment. He was picking up the ice skates and gesturing for Ailsa to sit down on the Abbey wall, presumably so he could strap them onto her feet.

'In answer to that,' he said eventually, concentrating on the fastenings, 'it wasn't just the riding. It wasn't just Jacob. You remember he was the cousin who witnessed it all? Lydia's future husband? There's actually a stronger argument for how he felt about Ella — he loved her, almost to distraction. Dangerously so, in fact.

'So it wasn't just the storm that nobody could have predicted, because nobody could have stopped that anyway. Much of it was Ella being the wonderful bloody-minded, stubborn, person she was. Or *is*, rather — because we're in her life, remember. She's a very determined girl — and if you imagine some sort of scales, with all the different factors weighing up and the end result being what happened to her, you can perhaps imagine what would happen if you took one factor away.

'If she was an excellent horsewoman, she could have gone out that night and tried to jump a fence to take a shortcut and had an accident anyway. If you keep Jacob away — remember, if you will, that he was actually trying to help, in his own way; he was trying to tell her not to go too near the edge of the cliff, but she couldn't hear his warnings — it might, just might, have triggered something far more dangerous in him, a desperation of sorts. Then Ella might have suffered far more than she did.

'What I'm trying to say, is that it was pre-destined. It would have happened and nothing could have stopped it. We can't rewrite history. History happened. This is real — we're here with them — but what happens next year will happen regardless, by fair means or by foul. We have to let it ride out. And I don't like it any more than you do. But at least, for now, and even right up until it happens, they are happy.' He wiggled her foot gently, making sure the skate was on securely, then did the same with the other foot. 'There — is that all right, my love?'

'Yes.' Ailsa was still trying to take it all in, and she moved her feet almost mechanically. 'So we can't help?'

'We shouldn't even try to. And I have to warn you — ' Ned smiled up at her but there was a hint of steel in his eyes ' — like I said, I'll know when you try and I *will* stop it. Are you ready to stand up?'

She quailed a little bit under his gaze. 'I think so.' She pushed herself off the wall and balanced herself on the blades. 'I still don't like not helping her.'

Ned made sure she was steady enough to leave alone, then sat down and deftly fastened on his own skates. 'I'm not in the business of preventing death or destruction. That's a very specific job and the responsibility of a Guardian Angel or whatever people like to call them. For me, I prefer to work on the principle of soulmates; finding them, knowing them, keeping them close. Now.' He stood up and put his hands on his hips. 'Time to go and get trounced by our friends.' He held a hand out and raised his eyebrows.

Before Ailsa could question him or even dwell further on anything he had told her, she found herself hobbling over to the frozen pond, hand in hand with Ned. Adam had managed to get a blaze going and the horse was munching quite happily on a pile of carrots that had been produced from somewhere — probably the box in the back of the sleigh.

Lydia and Ella were fastening each other's skates on amidst much giggling and Adam was doing the same. He'd sat just a little distance from Ella, and Ailsa saw their two heads bent to the task in hand — Adam's fair hair, tousled and adrift from driving the sleigh and Ella's honey-coloured curls escaping from her hat.

Adam looked up first and his gaze settled on Ella. As if she could feel it, she looked up and across at him, then blushed and smiled, casting her eyes down, then peeping back up at him. Adam was just staring at her, his smile widening as she noticed him. Their eyes locked and neither of them made a move to look away.

Ailsa wished she could frame that moment in time; capture it forever — the pair of them, seeing each other as if for the first time.

God, she wished she had her smartphone with her. That was a photo opportunity if ever she saw one.

'That's it,' whispered Ned. 'That's

the moment we wanted. I think they both know for sure now — it's something to build on. Hurrah at last.'

Then, shattering the moment: 'All right. Let's start!' That was Lydia. She stood up and hurried over to the Abbey pond, testing the ice gently with the toe of her boot, her arms out to the side as if she was doing a particularly elegant ballet pose. 'It seems just right. Me first!' She glided onto the ice and turned a perfect pirouette. 'Oh this is wonderful! What a marvellous idea!' She skated off and began to do circuits of the pond, interspersed with figure of eights.

Ailsa could only stand and stare in awe. 'She's amazing!' she whispered to Ned.

'Adam did warn you,' he said. 'Come on — we have to embarrass ourselves at some point. Might as well make it sooner rather than later.'

He stepped onto the ice and wobbled, his hand clutching hers more tightly as he tried to get his balance. Ailsa couldn't help it; she started laughing and stepped onto the ice herself. She wobbled even more than Ned did and the laughter turned into a shriek of horror as she found herself sitting down on the pond, still hanging onto Ned as she brought him down too.

'Oh God, I'm so sorry!' she cried and tried to stand up.

'My fault. It was my fault!' he said, laughing. They leaned on each other and managed to scramble to their feet, only to fall over again in a tumble of petticoats and overcoat.

'This is awful!' she shouted. 'I told you! I told you!'

'I told you as well!'

'We're dreadful! Oh God! Oh no. Oh Ned!'

'Good Lord. Come on — up you get — *whoaaaah!* Down you go.'

It seemed to be the pattern of the direness that was unfolding, ice-skating on the Abbey pond. It took a good while for Ailsa and Ned to get their balance, and culminated in them shuffling slowly along the ice, very close to the edge, their arms wrapped around each other and Ailsa wanting, terribly, to burst into silly giggles.

Lydia weaved her way between the four of them — Ella and Adam, and Ailsa and Ned — mocking them all delightedly for their failure at skating. 'Honestly, you get just as much practice as I do — why are you all so *slow*?' she crowed as she unbalanced Ned just by skating up to him then shooting away at a sharp angle. 'Look at those two — it's simply hysterical.' She pointed to their companions and grinned.

Ella was gliding stiffly, her arms stuck out to the sides and her face a study of deep concentration. Adam was doing slightly better, his arms behind his back, going slowly but at least remaining upright for longer than the rest of them.

'Oh!' Suddenly, there was a ladylike yelp from the opposite side of the pond and Ella went sprawling backwards, sitting down with a thump on the ice.

'Ella!' Adam sped up and wobbled as fast as he could across the ice. He bent down and put his fingers gently under her chin, tilting her face up towards him. 'Are you all right? You're not hurt?'

'No — no, I'm not hurt.' Ella lifted her hands from the ice and rubbed them together, dusting ice from her gloves. 'I'm just embarrassed.'

'There's nothing to be embarrassed about. Look at Ned and Ailsa. I think they've spent most of the time on the ground as well.'

'Oh, you're all so hopeless!' Lydia was almost crying with laughter and pointing to them on the ground. 'You're hereafter known as the Lord and Lady of Misrule!' she declared.

She spun around and around, showing off more of her pirouetting skills, dotting in between them and being thoroughly obnoxious, until Adam had enough and shouted, 'Whatever do you mean by that?'

'The Lord of Misrule presides over

the Feast of Fools and is in charge of the Christmas revelries!' cried Lydia. 'His Lady obviously does the same. You're certainly making me laugh, and you all look incredibly foolish. You're — oh!' Lydia tumbled to the ground and sat there looking indignant.

'I'm dreadfully sorry,' said Ella, innocently. 'I don't know what happened there. I was trying to stand up and I must have just flung my leg out at a very peculiar angle.'

'You tripped me up!' said Lydia. 'Now why would you do that?'

'Because I'm the Lady of Misrule and I'm in charge of revelries,' said Ella. 'And you had to look foolish somehow.'

'You horror!' shrieked Lydia.

She began to scramble to her feet, but Ella tugged sharply at her skirt and pulled her down again. 'Oh my. Can't you stay upright? How awful.'

'Ella!' Lydia skidded across the ice on her bottom to get out of her way, but Ella got onto all fours and began to scrabble after her. The pair of them ended up rolling onto the snowdrift at the edge of the pond, almost crying with laughter. Adam half-marched, half-skated to the tumble of fur-trimmed frocks, blonde hair and skates that the girls had turned into. He ploughed into the middle of them and started trying to separate them, pulling his sister off Ella, then trying to keep Ella from darting around the side to tweak Lydia's hat or tug at her skirts.

Ailsa stared, fascinated. 'Were they always like this?' she whispered to Ned.

'For as long as I've known them,' he said wryly. 'Why?'

'You see the photographs and the paintings and things and think the Victorians were dreadfully stuffy and never smiled. Yet these three — ' She gestured to them. Adam yelled as he was pulled onto the ground and Lydia made off with his scarf, waving it like a banner as she danced off on the skates, as elegant as she had been on the ice.

'People don't really change,' Ned

said, smiling down at her. 'That's the beauty of my job. I see it all. Remember, you told me yourself — what we see in the pictures is just a moment frozen in time. They were real people, living and breathing and laughing and loving as we do. They're human. Or terrible specimens of humans, as these girls are!' He laughed, watching them. 'Poor Adam. Come on — time to break it up!'

By the time Ned and Ailsa had skated inexpertly towards the edge of the pond and stumbled onto the snow, Lydia had bounded into the midst again and was trying to relieve Adam of his hat. It was starting to get quite cold now Ailsa had stopped moving and the winter sun was dropping.

'Hoi! We've had enough!' shouted Ned towards the tangle of limbs and people. 'My coat is soaked and my wife is frozen half to death.' He was ignored as the spectacle continued. 'Hey! Ahoy there!' he tried again.

'It's not working,' said Ailsa. 'I think

we might need to try a different tactic.'

'Oh? And what do you suggest, Mrs Cavendish?'

'It sounds so odd when you call me that!'

'But I have to call you that — and to be honest, I *want* to call you that.' Ned turned to her and looked down, his eyes full of humour. 'It's got a certain ring to it, don't you think?'

'Now stop teasing me — we've only been married a couple of hours! It's difficult for me to get used to it.' Ailsa laughed and bent down. She scooped up a handful of snow and began to form it into the semblance of a ball. 'Here. I'm a rotten shot.'

She handed the snowball over to Ned who took it and raised his eyebrows. 'An excellent idea, Mrs Cavendish,' he said. He weighed it in his hands and took aim. He threw it, perfectly straight, as if he had bowled in County Cricket matches all his born days.

The snowball landed right in the middle of the tussle and Lydia shrieked as it exploded all over her. 'Who did that? Who did that?'

Lydia, Ella and Adam broke apart, Adam keeping his hand on Ella's arm just a little longer than necessary as he steadied her back on her feet.

'It was Ailsa. Now — are we ready to get warm?' shouted Ned, waving at them. 'Two minutes by the fire as we get these dratted skates off, and dry out a little, please!'

'You liar! I didn't throw that at all!' cried Ailsa, spinning around to face him. She turned back to their friends. 'It was Ned, I promise!'

'She made it!' retorted Ned.

'He threw it!'

'She — ouch!' Ned uttered as a clumsily made snowball exploded on his chest and a flurry of soft snow flew up into his face.

'Oh dear.' That was Ella, clapping her hands across her mouth and staring at them. 'I'm so very sorry. I didn't actually mean to hit you.' She looked up at Adam as if worried that he would find that behaviour a step too far. Instead, he laughed and patted her on the shoulder.

He looked down at her, his eyes warm and admiring in his handsome face. 'Very impressive, Ella. All those summers of me teaching you cricket on the lawn have paid off.'

'But that's not fair!' Lydia cried. 'I was never any good at bowling. You all have an unfair advantage. Ned always made me field — I always had to stand in the corner.'

'Best place for you,' commented Adam.

'Now, now, don't give all my secret strategies away,' said Ned. He linked arms with Ailsa and they hobbled over to the group. Ailsa was trying to process all the information and was, in actual fact, just getting herself into a knot.

Ned obviously knew this family a lot better than she realised. Or it was all, perhaps, part of this weird dream.

'Cricket?' she asked quietly.

'Played a lot when I was a boy,' he

replied. Then he raised his voice. 'No, Lydia — no — don't do it. Yes. You missed. And that's why you were always fielding. Go into the corner — now, please!' A second soft snowball broke up in the air and scattered bits of snow about six feet away from Ned's feet.

'Oh it's a silly game,' grumbled Lydia, folding her arms.

'It is,' agreed Ned. 'So let's get these skates off and head back to the Park. I've told Ailsa about the mince pies and mulled wine that should be waiting for us.'

'Oh! Mince pies! Mulled wine!' Lydia cheered up immediately and deftly wrapped Adam's scarf around her neck. 'Yes! Let's go back. Ella — come on, darling.' She held her hand out to her friend, whose nose was pink and her hat askew.

'Thank you.' Ella took Lydia's hand and then, arm-in-arm, they stamped over on their skates to the fire which was burnt down considerably by now. Still, it had enough heat left in it for them all to huddle around and help each other off with the skates, fumbling and complaining about their stiff fingers and their clothing, heavy with melted snow.

Ailsa thought she had never had such a perfect outing.

★   ★   ★

Ned and Adam, finally satisfied that the horse was bridled correctly, went over to the fire and threw snow over it to dampen it down.

'That was quite a success for your sister,' said Ned as they stood before the guttering flames and watched them hiss and spit as they died, until there was nothing but a thin plume of smoke coming from the charred wood.

'I'm awfully sorry she dragged you both into it,' said Adam. He held his hands out over the remains of the fire, hoping, perhaps to get the last little bit of heat out of it. 'I'd quite forgotten how bad you were at ice-skating.'

'I never improve,' said Ned wryly. 'But it's been exactly the sort of thing that Ailsa wanted to do, so I'm very grateful to Lydia.'

'I suspect your wife thought she'd come here and have a nice, restrained Christmas Eve. Instead, she falls down several times, gets soaked through and experiences a couple of hoydens cat-fighting. I hope she doesn't judge us too harshly!'

'I'm sure she doesn't judge you at all,' replied Ned. He rubbed his own hands together. 'I often wish that snow was warmer.'

'I know exactly what you mean. Still, I'm determined to enjoy myself this Christmas. I have to go away to warmer climes just afterwards. The agents in France aren't too happy with some of the terms the merchants have offered us. It needs to be resolved.' Adam pulled a face and stared into the dark patch on the ground. The snow had melted all around and grass was poking through for the first time in days. 'I don't want to go, particularly, but there you are. I have a business to run, after all.'

'You'll miss Ella,' said Ned.

Adam looked at him quickly. 'I'll miss Lydia as well, of course.'

'Of course,' replied Ned, 'but we can all see where your heart really lies.'

Adam stared at him, his face reddening. 'Just because you're now a married man, there's no need to accuse us all of giving our love so lightly!'

'I never gave it to her lightly,' said Ned with a laugh. 'She was like a comet, blazing towards me. I couldn't have avoided her, even if I'd tried.'

'Pretty words, my friend. I see marriage has made you soft,' said Adam with a laugh. 'I wish you luck in it, though, I do, most sincerely. Myself, I doubt she'd even consider it. We grew up together, for God's sake!'

'You might be surprised,' said Ned, clapping his friend on the back. 'I suggest you take the opportunity of your forthcoming business trips to reflect and consider. For example, can you see either of you settling with anyone else?'

Adam looked back at the fire and shrugged. 'For my part, no. But for hers — who knows?'

'Reflect and consider, my friend. Reflect and consider. Now — we had best get back before the hoydens escape and drag us back on to the ice.'

The men turned their backs on the fire and began to walk back to the sleigh.

'I do hope they don't want to go back onto the ice,' said Adam. 'I can't ever remember being so cold before!'

'It's not the most pleasant feeling,' Ned agreed. He thrust his hands in his pockets and shook his damp hair out of his eyes. 'At least, though, I still have my scarf.'

'Lucky you,' said Adam. He looked towards the sleigh and nodded at Lydia. 'Tell you what, old chap, I'll sell you my sister. How about that? Perhaps it'll raise a little capital for the French investors.'

Ned laughed. 'No thank you. I could never keep up with her schemes and whims.'

Adam sighed. 'That would make two of us then. Come on, let's hurry back before it really does get too dark and too cold for sensible mortals to be outside.'

'Sensible mortals.' Ned smiled. 'Quite so.' And he pushed his hands further into his pockets and hurried towards the sleigh, towards Ailsa.

★ ★ ★

Ailsa had helped to toss the skates into the box on the back of the sleigh, and stood waiting whilst Lydia and Ella dragged even more blankets out of it.

The three of them tucked more blankets around each other as they sat and waited for Adam and Ned. Ella was sitting next to Ailsa, facing forwards, and Ailsa could see the consternation in her beautiful blue eyes as she concentrated on Ned and Adam.

'The poor boys,' said Ella, 'I feel dreadful that we have the blankets and they don't.' She shrank down amidst the tartan, apparently following the conversation as the men headed across to them in a way that only she could do; then she watched them as they harnessed the horse, blowing on their fingers and fastening buckles that refused to comply.

'Oh it's no good,' she said softly. She unwrapped herself and sat upright. 'Adam. Here. Take this blanket. Tuck it over your legs as you drive. You must be frozen.'

'But I'm perfectly warm, Ella,' he said, looking surprised.

'No, you're not,' she replied. 'You told Ned you can't ever remember being so cold before. Here. Take it.'

Adam stared at her, then shook his head in despair. 'I would protest and deny it, but I never could get anything past you, could I?'

'Never,' she agreed, frowning at him, her mouth set in a little stubborn line.

Adam protested anyway. 'But you're

cold and damp yourself, Ella.' He raked his hand through his hair and looked at her in despair.

'Not as cold as you.'

'Ella . . .'

Ailsa's heart jumped as she saw an opportunity she *could* take. She put her hand on Ella's arm. Ella turned to her, still looking, it had to be said, a little stubborn.

'Why don't you compromise?' Ailsa suggested. 'You travel upfront with Adam. You can watch where you're going and he can share the blanket.'

'Pardon?' Ella stared at her. 'What? I travel up there?' She pointed to the driver's seat. 'With the blanket?'

'And with Adam,' said Lydia, slyly. She'd wrapped Adam's scarf around her head so she resembled a Russian peasant woman. It didn't look as if her brother was going to get his scarf back this side of Christmas.

A look of confusion passed across Ella's face, as if she wanted to ride upfront, but didn't want to admit it.

'That's a good idea,' said Ned. He smiled at Ailsa and his dark eyes softened. 'That's something we *can* do here today.'

Ailsa sat back, and snuggled inside her blanket, feeling ridiculously warm inside — even if her nose *was* dropping off and she couldn't feel her face anymore. At last, she'd meddled in their lives in a way he'd supported.

'Come on, Ella. Out you get.' Ned held out his hand before the girl could complain, and helped her elegantly out of the sleigh.

'But it's high,' she said, looking up at where she was going to sit, as if that was the final thing she could say to change anyone's mind.

'It's not that high,' said Adam. 'Hold onto this — that's it.' He made sure she took hold of one of the metal curls that formed the frame of the sleigh and put his hands gently around her waist to lift her up.

Once she was up there, Ella turned to face Lydia and Ailsa, her hands clutching the back of the seat. 'But — '

'Here's a blanket,' said Lydia, passing one up to her and pushing it into her friend's hands. 'Take it. Tuck yourselves up. There now. How marvellous.'

Lydia turned back to face Ailsa and winked broadly, implying full well that Ella would have to complain to the back of her head and wouldn't be able to argue very effectively.

Ned climbed in to the sleigh — beside Ailsa, this time — and she moved the blanket to accommodate them both beneath it. They were supposed to be newlyweds after all. There wasn't anything wrong with sharing a tartan blanket, was there? And besides, Ned felt warm and safe and solid beside her.

And it would have been a much colder journey home had he not raised his arm and had she not snuck underneath it and been drawn in towards him, where she could feel his steady breathing and the beat of his heart beneath his scratchy waistcoat.

* * *

They were much quieter on the way back from the Abbey than they had been on the way. Ailsa was pleased to see that Ella and Adam had moved closer together — one blanket around their knees and one around their shoulders — but whether it was by accident or design or by instinct alone, she didn't know.

At one point, Ella was holding the reins, giggling while Adam tried to show her how to guide the horse. She was, admittedly, even quite bad at driving the sleigh, and certainly didn't like the idea of flicking the whip to encourage the horse. She clearly left that to Adam who kept trying to hand it to her, and she kept shaking her head emphatically and jiggling the reins instead.

Lydia seemed to be allowing the exercise and the fresh air and the warmth of the blankets to lull her into a daydream as she stared, her eyes glazed and unfocused, at the moors. They bounced over a rut and she started, then looked up at the sky. The sun was dropping and the clouds were silvery and gathering in low, and almost on cue a couple of flakes of snow drifted down and settled on the blanket.

'I think we left at the right time,' she said. 'We'll take the sleigh around to the courtyard and we can go in through the back door. We can kick off our boots and drop the skates off in the boot room and it'll be warm down there anyway. I might even steal a mince pie on our way past the kitchens.' Her eyes sparkled like the frost that was beginning to tip the hills and valleys of the snow drifts and ruts in the road.

'Is that where Ella's fountain is?' asked Ailsa, remembering the description of it in the book.

'Ella's fountain? Do you mean that old angel thing?' Lydia frowned, questioningly.

Too late, Ailsa remembered that the fountain had been in a state of disrepair until Adam had fixed it for Ella as a wedding gift. And, even worse, she recalled that it had subsequently been destroyed on their wedding day by, so the story went, a jealous Jacob. Oh she was *so* glad he wasn't here for Christmas! She didn't think she could have demonstrated much Victorian restraint with that man, despite what Ned had told her.

'Oh — well, it was just that — ' *Thank goodness!* She suddenly recalled a reason she could justify discussing it. ' — You said earlier that she loved the fountain and Adam had found her there when she was upset.' Her cheeks burned, embarrassed to think of that little scenario.

'Oh. Yes.' Lydia's eyes slid across the landscape again. 'That's right. Yes. The fountain is there. You'll be able to see it. Not that there's much to see. I don't know why she likes it so much.' The girl's eyebrows knitted together again and she shrugged the blanket further around her. Ailsa definitely got the impression that Ella's problems had affected Lydia more than she cared to admit, even to herself.

'Still, I'd like to see it,' replied Ailsa.

'You can't really miss it,' said Lydia. She turned and shouted to Adam. 'Straight into the courtyard, Adam.'

'Right-ho!' replied Adam, and spurred the horse on a little faster as the snow began to fall more heavily.

It wasn't long before they were skirting around the edge of the parkland and pulling up to the gate which led towards the back of the house. Adam slowed the horse down and Ailsa got a view of the back of Carrick Park she had never seen before. The structure and shape were the same, of course — but where the hotel had fenced off rubbish bins and skips, and where there were loading bays for suppliers and the VIP car park, and where it was just a tarmac square in the twenty-first century, there was a snow-covered area with a stone fountain in the middle of it.

Outbuildings seemed to embrace the

courtyard — a dairy, a laundry, a still room, perhaps — and a bench was placed, its back to the house, facing the fountain, piled up high with glittering, frosted snow.

The fountain was almost unrecognisable as an angel under the drifts of snow that clung to its wings and decorated its outstretched hands, but Ailsa knew beneath the smooth mounds of winter was a sweet face and loose curls of carved hair. The angel was, if you believed the story, a fair likeness of Ella.

'Happy now?' whispered Ned in her ear. 'Happy you've seen the angel fountain?'

'Yes,' replied Ailsa. 'I would have liked to see it without the snow though.'

'That can be arranged,' he said. 'Adam! Just stop here, would you — there's a good chap.'

'I'll have to get my assistant to slow the beast down,' called Adam. 'Ella. Pull on the reins — yes — just like that. *Whoah!* Whoah there, boy.' The horse stopped and pranced a little, shaking its mane, probably knowing that it wouldn't be long before it was back in the stables getting warmed and fed and rubbed down.

'He stopped!' cried Ella, delighted. 'I think I'm certainly a better driver than I am a horsewoman.'

'If you think so,' said Adam, amused. 'There you are, my friend. Stopped just at the fountain. Next thing, we offload the cargo and I take this sleigh back to the stables.'

'One thing, before you do that,' said Ned. He threw the blanket off and leapt down from the sleigh. He hurried over to the fountain and, before anyone could stop him, he had climbed up and jumped inside the base, sinking into the snow right the way up to his calves. He swore, to the delight of Lydia who clapped her hands and crowed with laughter, then he lifted his hands and began to sweep the snow off the angel, dusting it away from her face and her hair, knocking it off her wings and brushing it off her robes.

'There you are, Mrs Cavendish,' he cried, turning and throwing his arms out to the sides. 'One snow-free angel for your delight.' He swept a low bow, still standing inside the fountain base, and came up grinning. 'I know how much you wanted to see her face!'

'She looks like Ella! She does!' cried Ailsa. 'I can't believe it!'

'Believe it,' said Ned. 'It's Christmas Eve. You're allowed to believe in angels.'

'I believe in angels all the time,' said Ella, leaning forwards, her beautiful smile lighting up her face as she studied the fountain. 'Not just at Christmas. That's why I love this one so much.'

'Then you are a very sensible woman,' replied Ned, sweeping another bow to her. 'Now. If someone would be kind enough to help me get out of this thing, I would be most appreciative.'

There was a scramble as Lydia and Ailsa tossed off their own blankets and half-slid, half-clambered out of the sleigh, laughing. Ned threw his arms out again and beckoned them forward.

He gave one hand to each woman and managed to climb out of the bowl. His trousers were dripping wet and Ailsa didn't want to think about how soaked his feet must be.

'Thank you,' she said to him as Lydia released him and he turned to Ailsa and tucked her arm into his. 'I know it's true now. The story about Ella's angel. It's beautiful.'

'You're very welcome,' he said. 'And I'm bloody freezing.' His teeth were chattering and she could feel him shivering. 'It's tough being married to you. I have to do all these things to keep you happy.'

'Surely I'm worth it,' she teased as they made their way towards the back door.

'I wouldn't have it any other way,' he replied. He stood back and let her in first. Ailsa waited, just inside, for him to stamp off the worst of the snow, and looked out at the angel. The courtyard was a mess of footprints and sleigh tracks and hoof prints, and there were clumps of snow, fallen from the fountain, ruining the pristine appearance of it all. She thought she had never seen it look more lovely.

Ella was hurrying in behind them and Lydia was bringing up the rear, four pairs of skates dangling from her fingertips. She was shouting some instructions to Adam as she headed towards the warmth.

'Adam is taking the sleigh back to the stables,' Ella told Ailsa. 'I said I would come with him to see Blackie, but he said I was too wet and needed to get indoors. I'll go up later and take him a treat for Christmas.'

She was shivering too and Ailsa moved aside. 'You'll take Adam a treat or Blackie a treat?' she asked.

'Oh! Ha! Blackie. Of course.' Ella giggled. 'Adam will probably get a treat from Johnson. He's the head stable hand, and I do think he spoils Blackie more than anyone. He is also fond of whisky and I'm sure Adam will be inveigled into having a festive drink with him.'

Ella headed into a room just to the side of the corridor and dropped her own skates on the floor. She grabbed a button hook from the scrubbed wooden table and bent down to start undoing her boots.

She looked up and smiled at Ailsa. 'I'll help you with yours if you would like me to. I'm used to doing them myself from living with my aunt, but I know Lydia prefers someone to help her. I don't mind.'

Ella, then, was still quite down to earth. She certainly wasn't some Victorian diva that shouted until she was heard.

'That would be lovely,' said Ailsa. She didn't want to show her ignorance by failing to undo the boots. 'I always take far too long and I'm desperate to get them off.'

'I don't blame you,' said Ella. 'Please — sit down. I'll do them.'

Ailsa sat and watched Ella work. She bit down on her lip hard. She'd only known Ella a short time, but it was so unfair. *Life* was so unfair.

She felt the pressure of Ned's hand on her shoulder, squeezing it. It was either a reassuring squeeze, or a warning squeeze. She reached up and covered his hand briefly with hers.

'I know,' she murmured, safe in the knowledge that Ella had her head bent to the task in hand and wouldn't read her. 'I'll say nothing.'

The pressure left her shoulder, then he patted it. He came around into view and leaned against the table, pulling his own boots off. He upended the first one and water spilled out of it.

'Rather damp,' he said, repeating the process with the other one.

By now, Ella had finished and sat back on her heels. 'All done,' she said. 'I'll do Lydia next. She'll be ordering those mince pies in the kitchens.'

'Indeed I was,' said Lydia, sweeping into the little room, which was now starting to get quite crowded. 'Thank you my dear. Ned, I'll see you in twenty minutes as we agreed? In the hallway?'

Ella looked from one to the other. 'You're making him go out again?' she asked, surprised.

'It's a job he promised he would help me with,' said Lydia. Ailsa stood up and moved so Lydia could take the seat. Lydia pulled her skirt up and stuck her foot out, ready for the button hook. 'But he needs to change into dry clothes first.'

'Ned, you'll freeze. You can't go back out there!' interjected Ailsa.

'Ah, my wonderful wife,' said Ned, dropping a kiss on her forehead. 'How nice that you worry about me. But I'll be perfectly all right. I'll see you as we arranged, Lydia. And you, Ailsa Cavendish, can relax for a little while. I'll see you in about an hour. I'm just going to find some dry clothes.' He put his hands in his pockets, and left the room, looking incongruously modern in the old-fashioned boot room.

Ella tapped Ailsa's hand so she looked at her. 'It's all right. This place is like a rabbit warren. I'll take you back through to the main part of the house.'

Ailsa knew she would find her way no problem. The old servants' staircase was a fire escape route in the hotel, and a short cut down to the ground floor for the staff after all.

But she bit her lip again and nodded and smiled at Ella Dunbar as if she was the guest she was supposed to be.

*   *   *

It didn't take Ned long to change into a warm, dry suit, and he was waiting in the hallway for Lydia as promised.

Lydia ran down the stairs, now wearing a heavy cloak over her outfit and obviously ready to head back out into the snow. 'Thank you. Did I keep you waiting? Poor Ned!'

'You're here now. But you've only got yourself to blame if it gets too dark to find what we want.'

'It's still daylight. We have hours yet!' cried Lydia.

'Maybe not hours!' replied Ned. 'But

come on — let's go, then we can get back inside.'

'I do appreciate you coming with me,' said Lydia, smiling up at him, her eyes mischievous. 'It's something I need to do before Adam goes away.' She hurried towards the main door and stood back for Ned to open it for her. 'I just think we're running out of time.' She stood on the steps and looked so guileless that for a moment Ned wondered if she knew more of the future than he thought.

'What do you mean?' he asked carefully.

'I mean,' said Lydia twirling away from him and running down the steps, 'that Adam is going to Europe soon, and he still hasn't set his cap at Ella. Any idiot can see they're meant to be together. Any idiot, except my brother who is the biggest idiot I know.'

'Ah. I see.' Ned blew out a little *huff* of air, relieved. It was a long time since he had come across anyone who knew more about the futures of the people he helped than he did; and he seriously doubted Lydia was privy to that sort of information, but he needed to be sure.

'So, Ned, as one of his oldest friends — who has, I must say, managed to find a wonderful woman of his own — I need your advice.' Lydia stopped in the middle of the driveway, snowflakes falling and settling on her cloak, her cheeks and nose still pink from the sleigh-ride. 'What's the best thing to do? Or are we hoping for something that's never going to happen?'

'I think it'll happen,' said Ned, 'but I think we need to speed it up a bit. Now — it's Christmas. And I think your idea, Lydia Carrick, is perfectly wonderful.'

Lydia jumped up and down, clapping. 'Marvellous. Now — let's head to the woods. That's probably the best place isn't it?' She was off, running away before him like an excited child.

Ned cast a glance back at the house. In the morning room window, he saw a shadow. The height and the shape suggested to him that it was Ailsa. He knew he had to get back to Carrick Park as soon as he could — and not just because he wanted to spend as long as he could and as long as he dared with the dark-haired beauty he had, this time, seen in the drawing room of Carrick Park.

His glance slid across to the strip of ocean he could see in the far distance; then he turned away from that and strode after Lydia, hunched up in his coat and very glad that he had managed to save his own scarf from the hoydens earlier.

5

1864

After changing into the dry clothes that someone had helpfully left out on her bed, and summoning Elizabeth again, to help her undress and dress, Ailsa had spent the past hour exploring the house.

She'd looked at the books in the library, stood in the centre of the morning room and popped her head into the study, seeing the rooms she knew, yet didn't know in this world. She'd also leaned on the window sill of the morning room, and stared out, trying to spot familiar landmarks, but all she could really pick out was the strip of sea across the moors. No telegraph poles or lines broke up the view. And she didn't think she'd ever seen it quite so snowy and quite so white in all the years she had worked at the hotel.

Somewhere, there might be little roads or tracks across the moors, quite impassable without the help of a friendly farmer and his tractor or a snow plough. She shivered. It was quite isolating, when you thought about it. And for someone like Ella, it must have been terrifying the morning she stood in the servants' corridor and willed a bell to sound loud enough for her to hear.

Perhaps she had run outside and stood in the courtyard, straining to catch the call of a gull or a song of a thrush; a gust of wind as it whipped past her or the distant chime of a church bell. And there was nothing. How absolutely horrific. She had been, Lydia had said, about seventeen when it happened — just at the point in her life where she should have been getting excited about balls and parties. And then to have Adam, all those years, in love with her — and only to grab that chance a few months before she died . . . before they both died; for hadn't Adam gone as well? No. As beautiful and as captivating and as seemingly privileged as Ella was, Ailsa knew now she would not have traded places with her. Not even for all those wonderful Christmases in Carrick Park.

A vision of Ned flitted into her mind; his pale face and his dark hair and his dark, dark eyes. If she, for instance, met someone who she thought could mean everything to her, would she know? Would she grasp the chance with both hands and love that person as much as she dared, for as long as she could?

She had taken those dreary and frightening thoughts to her bedroom — tried, more to the point, to make sense of this whole thing. If it was a dream, it was an awfully long and detailed dream, and far too philosophical for the middle of the night. She had dozed off for fifteen minutes or so, as she lay on the soft bed, looking at the ceiling, tracing the plasterwork on the coving, lulled by the warmth of the fire and the solid tick-tock of the clock. She awoke with a start, expecting to see her usual Carrick Park ceiling in the servants' quarters, and to see the glow of her mobile phone on the bedside table. But no: she was still looking up at the intricate plasterwork and lying on a feather mattress, her satin skirts spread all around her, heavy against her legs.

After that, she had made her way downstairs, still feeling as if she was dreaming and was now sitting in the drawing room, in front of the fire, aching in places she didn't know she could ache. Someone had brought mulled wine in, decorated with a cinnamon stick and a plate of little mince pies. Lydia's instructions had been carried out with perfect timing. The pies were still hot from the oven, the wine warm and spicy and a delight to sip as she sniffed the mingled scents of cinnamon and pine resin from the huge Christmas tree.

She had already been up to the tree and adjusted the pretty china angel that Adam had lifted off earlier, and was now munching her way through the festive treats, her mind going over the day, still wondering if any of it was real — despite her muscles telling her it was — when the door opened with a soft *click*.

Ailsa looked up and saw Ella standing in the doorway, half-in, half-out of the room.

'Good afternoon.' Ella's voice was clear in the quiet room. She pressed her hands together in front of her skirt and smiled shyly at Ailsa.

'Good afternoon.' Ailsa smiled back, sitting up straighter. 'Do you want a mince pie? They're very nice. I might have to eat them all if you don't.'

'A mince pie? Oh — well. Maybe just one.'

'Come in then.'

'Thank you.' Ella smiled again and stepped inside the room. She shut the door behind her and leaned on it for a moment. 'You don't mind me coming in and bothering you, do you?' she asked, a flicker of concern passing over her lovely face. 'It's been a busy day. Lydia always keeps us busy, but you might not be used to it. So you can tell me to leave if you want. I know you've had a long journey down to us today, without all the skating and everything.'

'Of course I don't mind. It's nice to see you. Please. Sit down. It's more your house than mine anyway. You don't have to ask my permission.'

Ailsa was conscious of Ella following her lips as she spoke and hoped she wasn't talking too fast. She knew some basic sign language, thanks to courses through work, but, even though there was just the two of them there, she thought it might be a little rude to try and start a conversation she might end up unable to finish.

'But it's not really my house, although it's always felt like mine. They make me very welcome. Lydia is like my sister. We bicker all the time but I love her dearly and I know she loves me. And Adam — well — Adam is . . . Adam.' She dipped her head momentarily, but couldn't hide the blush or the little smile from Ailsa. Ella looked back up, composing her expression into a more serious one. 'He's going away after Christmas and I'll miss him a great deal. We both will. He has to travel a lot for his business, and Lydia hates being alone. My aunt died recently and I've been here more or less constantly ever since.

'Lydia has said I can stay on as long as I want, but I know I'll have to go to my real home at some point. I'm supposed to live at York.' She pulled a face, the serious expression disappearing. She wasn't a girl, Ailsa had now realised, who could be too serious for too long; images of her misbehaving on the ice sprang into Ailsa's mind and she had to work to keep her own expression blank.

'*But*,' continued Ella, her eyes wide, 'the only thing I really *like* about our town house in York is the piano.'

'You've got a better piano here, though,' said Ailsa.

Ella smiled, without restraint this time, and it was like the room lit up. 'Indeed it is. *Much* better. And they don't mind me thrashing out my old Mozart. I must make a dreadful din.'

'I'm sure you don't,' said Ailsa. She pushed the tray of mince pies over to Ella, whose fingers hovered over them for a moment, before she selected one.

'I'm sure I do,' replied Ella. 'Adam says I play wonderful music but he's a liar.'

'No he's not.' Ailsa laughed. 'The carols were beautiful.'

'Which one is your favourite?' asked Ella, delicately licking the sugar off her fingers.

Ailsa thought quickly. It was safer to choose one of the ones Ella had played — she wasn't much good with when carols had been written and what if she chose one that had been written after 1864?

'I think it's *O Holy Night*,' she said

carefully. She did like it.

'*O Holy Night?*' Ella looked at her enquiringly. 'That one? Did I play it well enough for you?'

'It was perfect,' replied Ailsa. She couldn't help herself — she made the sign for 'perfect', just to drive her point home; both hands up in the air, her fingers spread apart and her thumb and forefingers making little circles.

There was a spark of interest in Ella's eyes and she nodded. *Thank you* she signed back; her own fingers spread, her fingertips tapping her chin and moving away, palm inwards, towards Ailsa.

Again, Ailsa thought her heart would break for this sweet, funny, loving girl who was so concerned for others, and who, being brutally honest, would be dead by next Christmas.

God, the thought was horrible. If she could only warn her —

'Ella — ' she started.

Then the door was flung open and Lydia tumbled in with Ned, clutching a sprig of mistletoe. 'Look! Look what we found! Mistletoe! You know what you have to do!'

Ella must have sensed a shadow fall over her, or felt the draught as the door opened, because she started and turned in her chair to face them. 'Lydia! What's that?'

'Mistletoe!' cried Lydia. She brandished it again. 'I just said!'

'Well maybe you did,' said Ella, pertly, 'but *I* didn't hear you.'

This time it was Ailsa's turn to look at the ground and hide a smile. You had to give the girl credit.

'That's always your excuse,' replied Lydia, 'but regardless it's mistletoe. Ned found it.'

Ella turned to face Ailsa and rolled her eyes. Slowly, she signed something to her.

I want to tell you how perfect for you Ned is. I see more than people think. He adores you. Make sure you love him always.

Ella looked questioningly at Ailsa and Ailsa nodded, dumbly.

I understand. Thank you.

Ella smiled and stood up. 'So what are we going to do with the mistletoe?' she asked.

Lydia began to describe where she thought it should go and Ned came over to Ailsa, letting Lydia run away with her ideas.

'What did she say?' he asked, his back to the girls so Ella, at least, couldn't read the conversation.

'Nothing important,' she said, her eyes sliding across to the door where Lydia was now demonstrating how she could hang the mistletoe there to catch people as they came in. 'Just something I'd been wondering about. But you knew we were here, didn't you? That's why you came in.' She looked back at Ned, challenging him with her eyes. 'You knew I was going to say something to her.'

'Do you think so?' he asked.

'I know so,' replied Ailsa. 'I know, I know. I can't and I shouldn't, but it's so hard.'

'You're not here to rewrite their history,' said Ned softly. He took her hand in his and kissed it. 'Let them be. It's something I have to fight against myself, but you'll learn.'

'I don't know if I do want to learn,' said Ailsa miserably. 'I'm in the business of helping people to make a life together. I can't just stand back and let them — *die*!'

'It's very hard,' replied Ned. 'Very hard indeed. But they have each other, right up until the end. Some things we just have to be grateful for. Anyway — '
In one, swift movement, he pulled Ailsa around so they were both facing the door. 'Good Lord!' Ned cried. 'She's only gone and fixed it up there! Come on, Mrs Cavendish. Let's test it out!'

And he drew her over to the doorway, took hold of her right there and then, and kissed her in full view of everyone.

He didn't just kiss her; it was one of those theatrical kisses where the man bends the lady over backwards and swoops down on her. Ailsa gasped and thought her corsets were sure to go *ping* under the strain. His hand was in the small of her back, her arms flailing wildly, until she reached up and hung onto his neck. She felt his hair curling under her fingertips, his skin warm against hers, the scent of winter and frost and pine clinging to his overcoat. Then, supporting her as if she were the most precious, most breakable thing in the world, he pulled her upright. His black eyes were sparkling with mischief, his lips tilted into the most captivating smile she'd ever seen.

'Oh my.' Her voice was a whisper, her cheeks burning. 'Now why did you go and do that, Ned Cavendish?'

'I told you that you might not appreciate my efforts to stop you talking about the future. But more than that, I did it simply because I love you and because the opportunity was too good to miss,' he answered, without shifting his attention from her. It was as if they were the only two people in the room and she was falling under some sort of spell — until there was a gleeful shout and a joyful clap from behind her.

'Edward Charles Cavendish!' cried Adam. 'You rake!'

Ailsa removed herself from Ned's embrace and turned towards her host, her face, she knew, scarlet, a million and one excuses on her tongue.

'Is it a free for all? Mistletoe, is it? Good *chap*, Lydia!' cried Adam. 'I came in at just the right time!' Suddenly, he grabbed Ella around the waist, bobbed his head to the side of hers so she could see him, then pulled the startled girl around to face him fully. Ailsa felt for Ella — she'd had no idea he was behind her and her face was a picture. She squealed and then, as she registered who it was, she began to giggle as her cheeks flushed rosy pink. 'Ha! Mistletoe. You can't escape now, Miss Dunbar,' Adam continued. He pulled her towards him and landed a kiss right on her mouth.

Ella's hands, her fingers spread like

starfish in shock, floundered a little like Ailsa's had; then they moved, hesitantly, up to Adam's shoulders. She closed her eyes, and returned the kiss; then they pulled apart, the pair of them staring at each other, apparently baffled. Reluctantly, it seemed, Ella removed her hands from Adam's shoulders and he released her waist. Almost as if it were choreographed, they both took half a step backwards. Their eyes, however, remained locked on one another.

Ailsa wanted to barge in and shout at the pair of them: *For God's sake — what are you doing? Do it properly! It's Christmas — people always get together at Christmas parties!*

But of course she didn't, possibly because she felt Ned's restraining hold on her own waist.

'I'm sorry.' That was Adam, talking to Ella. He smiled, shyly embarrassed and ran his hand through his hair. 'Johnson forced me into taking some whisky with him. It must have been stronger than I thought.'

'That's all right,' she said, a tiny wobble in her voice. 'There was mistletoe. You don't have to apologise. Please don't apologise.'

'Yes. Mistletoe,' replied Adam. 'The very stuff. And Johnson's whisky. More like Johnson's moonshine, I'll warrant. A terrible combination.'

Lydia was staring at the pair of them, her knuckles rammed in her mouth, her eyes wide. 'My goodness. That was wonderful,' she muttered around her knuckles. Ailsa cast a sharp glance at her. She clearly didn't want Ella to hear that comment.

Lydia must have felt Ailsa's eyes on her as she slid her own gaze around to meet her and smiled around her knuckles.

She moved her hand away slightly and whispered, 'For years and years I've tried to make that happen. And it did. I could honestly dance a jig. I'm so happy.'

Ailsa frowned at her. 'What do you mean?'

'Well almost everybody knows that those two are meant for each other except them. I really need to work on it a little more. I'll have to plan something.'

Ailsa thought she glimpsed a chance to change history. 'Well, you could — '

'You could just let it happen naturally,' interrupted Ned. He was smiling at Lydia, then he winked. 'Today has put the idea into their heads anyway.'

'I think the idea has always been there in both their heads,' said Lydia. She looked slyly across at her brother and her best friend, then moved so she had her back completely to Ella. 'But today is the first day we've ever come close to them admitting it to themselves — hurrah for mistletoe. It's so fortunate you found it, Ned!'

Ned smiled. 'Isn't it?' He had also turned away from the couple and he and Lydia were standing, indiscreetly, discussing Adam and Ella in such a position that there was no way Ella could have discovered what they were saying.

Not that either Adam or Ella would have noticed, anyway, thought Ailsa wryly; they were completely lost in one another.

Adam was busy talking to Ella about some random estate business, and she was nodding as if she was actually bothered about it all — but Ailsa saw that the pair of them were hot and flustered and Ella was nervously tucking hair behind her ear, and Adam's own hair was, by now, sticking out in tufts where he'd been raking his fingers through it.

God love them.

'At least now I have something to work on,' said Lydia with a wicked grin. 'I think I'll order some more mulled wine. It might just add to the whisky and fuel him into action — we can but hope.' She practically danced over to the bell-pull, leaving Ned and Ailsa alone before the fireplace.

And now, finally it had happened. 'I think my heart just broke a little bit,' Ailsa murmured.

'It shows you have one,' whispered Ned. 'It's nothing to be ashamed of.'

'I've seen enough,' said Ailsa, a catch in her voice. She turned to Ned, embarrassed to feel tears bubbling up, watching this fairy tale unfold, knowing how desperately, irrevocably, it would be broken by this time next year. 'I can't watch any more. If I stay, I won't be responsible for my actions. I'll say something or do something and tell them to stay away from here when that man comes.'

She referred, of course, to Jacob.

'You can't blame Jacob entirely,' said Ned softly. 'We've already had that conversation.'

'I can blame him enough.' She raised her hand and wiped a tear away. 'Can we go? Please?'

'Really?'

'Really.' She took a deep, shuddering breath and cast a glance at Ella, Lydia and Adam, clustered now by the door. She hadn't spent long with them, but she'd seen what she wanted to see. 'I wish it had all turned out well for them,' she said.

'I can grant most wishes,' replied Ned, taking her hand, 'but not everything is possible.' He leaned down and kissed her hand, then he led her over to the French doors, past the Christmas tree and away from the warmth of the fire.

'I do love the china angels,' Ailsa said in a small voice, deliberately coming to a halt beside the tree and looking up at it. 'And the candlelight. It's so pretty.'

'It's a beautiful tree. If not a little too tall. Lydia is a fiend for Christmas trees, but this is truly the worst fit yet.'

Ailsa gave a shaky little laugh, and allowed Ned to lead her through the French doors and out onto the frost-spangled terrace.

They stood, facing the rolling parkland and moors, the sea a strip of gunmetal in the distance, lit by the silver penny that hung above the horizon.

Snowflakes were falling and Ailsa closed her eyes, tilting her face up so they landed in sharp little dots on her face. 'Carrick Park has never changed, has it?' she asked.

'Never,' replied Ned. 'Are you sure you want to go back right now?'

'Yes. I'm guessing I'm a shadow anyway, and once I've gone, they'll never know I was here.'

'That's not quite how it works,' said Ned. 'You'll still be here — well, a version of you, anyway; a version who doesn't know anything beyond the here and now.'

'That sounds complicated,' replied Ailsa. She opened her eyes and stared out at the white landscape. 'How do I get back?'

'I'll take you,' he said. 'Like this.'

And he pulled her towards him, and he kissed her, and the world melted away and she wasn't aware of anything else for quite some time.

6

Christmas Present

When Ailsa opened her eyes, she was still clinging to Ned, still standing on the terrace and still facing a white landscape.

However, she was shivering in her pyjamas; there was a string of lights in the distance which marked a road, and moving lights were evidence of late night traffic trundling along it. A vague hum wormed into her consciousness as an aircraft flew overhead. And she could breathe properly. She wasn't wearing a corset, which had to be a blessing.

'We're back,' she said, looking around her. Ned still had her hands in his, she could still feel the warmth and the firm grip; but then, to her horror, she felt his grip relax and he let her hands drop.

'We are,' he said. 'Safe and sound. I'm glad that bit worked.'

His profile was stark against the wintry background, his face pale in the moonlight. His brows were knitted together and he appeared to be deep in thought — either that, or he was wrestling with some sort of inner demon.

Ailsa's stomach churned. She didn't quite understand — the day might have been a beautiful dream; it might have been real. She had no idea, but Ned had figured in her reality that Christmas Eve somehow. And she felt a draw to him that she didn't think she could ever explain. She didn't want to think beyond that — and she knew for a fact that she didn't want him to leave her. But she had a horrible feeling that that was going to happen.

'Will I see you again?' she asked, her heart thumping, dreading the answer. She wrapped her arms around herself. 'Or is this it?'

Ned put his hands in his pockets and his frown deepened, his eyes seeming to darken. Oh, how she just wanted to fall into those eyes and be done with it.

He shrugged. 'You'll be here next Christmas, won't you?' His voice was odd, clipped almost, as if he was saying words he didn't want to say, but he knew he had to. He didn't take his eyes off the distant horizon. The sea was still a slice of gunmetal; slate-grey, tipped with tiny specks of foam as the waves relentlessly crashed inland.

'I don't know.' Ailsa was thrown. 'All things being equal, then yes. I'll be here next year.'

'Good.' Ned nodded, still staring out to the coast. 'I'll see you then.' He turned and finally looked at her. He smiled down at her, his dark eyes burning into hers. 'I always come back for Christmas.'

'But I — '

'Listen!' He interrupted her, touching her gently on the arm. Her skin fizzed through the thin fabric and she almost expected to see sparks flying from where his fingertips lay. 'Do you hear that?' He nodded towards the French doors that led back into the drawing room.

'Oh! All I can hear is the clock chiming midnight. I didn't realise — '

'No — beneath that. Listen carefully.'

Ailsa tilted her head, and sure enough, beneath the chimes, she heard a different noise — a soft melody, played on a piano: *O Holy Night*.

Ailsa's heart began to pound. 'Ella!' she whispered, terrified that somehow the sound of her name would chase the girl away. 'I have to . . . '

She was almost unaware of Ned releasing her as she ran across the terrace. She flung the door open and ran into the room, her eyes fixed on the piano, her heart thumping fit to burst.

'Ella!'

But the room was empty, the last note still hanging in the air, as if Ailsa could simply reach out and touch it.

Useless tears sprang into her eyes and she bit her lip, looking around in case Ella, or whoever it was, had

157

scurried away into the shadows and was even now pressing themselves into the corner hoping they wouldn't be discovered. The atmosphere in the room shifted, as the last chime of midnight died away and Ailsa realised, desperately, that whatever magic might have been there, had faded.

'Merry Christmas, Ella,' she whispered. The words sounded odd in the empty room and Ailsa shivered. She turned back towards the French doors. There were still so many questions she wanted to ask Ned.

But when she got to the doors, they were locked firmly and the filmy material that served as curtains hung before them, undisturbed, not even waving in a breeze.

'Ned!' This time the name was almost shouted as she grabbed hold of the door and shook it. It remained fastened tight, the key turned in the lock from the inside. Fumbling, Ailsa wrenched the key around and pushed at the door, almost falling out onto the terrace.

The darkness pressed in on her and it was quite clear that she was alone. And even from here, as the lamplight spilled out into a little half-moon on the terrace, there wasn't a flake of snow anywhere to be seen; there was just damp, wet grass ahead of her, leafless trees, skeletal against the velvet sky, and the sea in the distance, the moonlight dancing across the waves.

Unbidden, Lydia's voice floated into Ailsa's mind: *Ned likes the view out to sea. I don't know why. He just says he likes to travel. I don't even know where he disappears to, he never tells us. But I'm sure you know where he goes.*

'I don't think I do,' whispered Ailsa. 'Not at all.' She looked around the drawing room, and blinked as it started to melt and fade. The darkness started coming in for her and, before she could do anything, she slid into a little heap on the floor, her eyes closed and her mind swarming with images from the day. The last thing she was aware of before she lost consciousness, was a breeze blowing in from the French doors and something that felt like the brush of angel wings: but it might just as easily have been a kiss as soft as a snowflake.

7

Christmas Morning

Present Day

Ailsa woke up in the narrow bed on the third floor and felt like she had the start of a headache. She'd been asleep for only a few hours, and she awoke with her mind churning over what had maybe been a dream, or what had, less likely, been some sort of Christmas reality that was too weird for words.

She was aching in her legs and bum and back, exactly as she would have been if she had indeed been ice-skating by the Abbey pond. But then again, it wasn't the world's most comfy mattress and it wasn't her own bed after all.

But it had been very, very realistic, that dream. She could have sworn she had spent a day with the Carricks. She sat up in bed and looked around the room, seeing the modern furnishings, the desk under the window with her iPad on it and the glow of her mobile phone next to her, a few minutes away from the alarm going off.

On the bedside table was the Becky Nelson Carrick Park book.

'Of course.' Ailsa blinked and shuffled over so her feet were on the ground. She'd been chatting to that guy last night and they'd started talking about the Carricks and the Christmases they must have experienced in Victorian times. It had all been on her mind — that and the bloody wedding today —

She checked herself. It was somebody's special day. She had no right to be grouchy over the fact she had to supervise it all for them on Christmas Day. But God, she could have done with a bit more sleep.

A vision flashed across her mind of standing on the terrace with the dark-haired man — Ned Cavendish. They'd been out there for some reason and she'd heard carols coming from the drawing room so she'd gone back in . . . She shook her head to clear it and scooped her hair back over her shoulder. That was Tara's fault, teasing her about the music.

It was all logical, but damn, it seemed real. She'd come straight up to her room after chatting to Ned and fallen into bed exhausted. And now, deep joy, she had to put her work clothes on and smile at a bride and groom, when all she wanted to do was analyse the dream.

Merry Christmas.

But never mind. It was her job, and she was paid to do it. So do it she would, and she'd do it with good grace. Sophie and Gabe were relying on her.

Christmas Night

The guests were still hanging around in the drawing room, Sophie and Gabe having long since departed to their suite. Ailsa was hovering in the corner, her legs aching, her smile fixed on her face as she nodded a goodnight to everyone and willed them all to leave so she could finish up the last few things and get the room returned to normal.

The only thing was, because she'd been so busy, she'd never had a great deal of time to think about Ned.

The more she considered him, though, the more questions it generated. Had it been real? Had *he* been real? Had the fact she'd fallen asleep reading the Carrick Park book meant she'd been dreaming the whole thing? His kisses and his touches and the sparks he generated whenever he touched her had seemed real enough. So had the sleigh ride and the ice-skating and the scent of that Christmas tree with the wonky top. She smiled as she remembered it.

She remembered also the mistletoe, hung over that very door *there*; and, more than any of it, she remembered how his kiss had felt as he took hold of her under the mistletoe bough, and how he had smelled of winter and frost and pine, and how his damp hair had curled under her fingertips, and how warm his skin was against hers.

She blushed furiously and dipped her head. Good grief. He was a wedding guest she'd met briefly last night; that was all, wasn't it? Although, if she thought very hard about it, had she even *seen* him today? Her attention had, she admitted, been on Gabe and Sophie; but surely Ned had been *somewhere*? Hadn't he?

Perhaps he had just stayed out of her way, hidden in the shadows in case he distracted her — goodness knew he wouldn't have to do much to distract her. One look, one smile and she'd not know if it was Christmas Day or Midsummer's Eve. The idea that he was simply a guest and her dreams had been more vivid than usual was what she had kept telling herself and what had carried her through the day.

She shifted position and the stiffness in her muscles told quite a different story — but it wasn't a story she thought she could believe.

* ★ ★

Ned stood on the cliff path near Whitby, overlooking the sea. He was at the ragged semicircle of bluff, which had crumbled away in that long-ago storm. He leaned his hands on the railings and looked out across the water. The sea was moving like molten mercury, heaving and rolling under the swell of the waves as they crashed onto the rocks and fell back onto themselves.

He had come here far too often, watching and wondering, trying not to let himself dwell on it. If he closed his eyes, he could see it still; the terrified girl in her green riding habit, her chubby little horse as panicked as she was. The lightning blasting across the night sky, the thunder making the very ground shake beneath his feet as he stood in the shadows, helpless, watching her attempt to control the animal.

Then there was Jacob — dark-haired, infatuated and passionately ruthless — appearing before her, jumping off his own horse to try and save her.

'*The cliff path is crumbling away, Ella,*' Jacob shouted, '*and the storm is too bad. It will not be safe. The rain . . .*'

He tried to signal what he meant, but she just shook her head again, close to tears. '*I cannot do it, Jacob; I cannot understand you. Please let me past. I need to find my husband.*'

Adam had gone to Whitby to see his solicitor — something to do with the estate, an appointment he'd arranged on their return from honeymoon. Ella, stubborn, beautiful Ella had insisted on riding with him, but the storm had come in with the evening, and she'd lost him, somewhere in the town. She'd tried to head back to the Park on Blackie, in the pitch dark of a November night. Jacob was there, following her secretively, trying to bring her back safely — and to hell with Adam.

But she'd been panic-stricken and hysterical and it had all gone wrong.

She tried to make the horse skirt

around him, but the gap was not very wide and the horse stumbled. Jacob grabbed the reins and pulled the animal towards him. Then he didn't know exactly what happened. One minute Ella was in the saddle, the next, apparently unseated by the horse's stumble, she was gone . . .

Ned dropped his head and stared at the edge of the cliff, inky, shiny black where it sheared away into nothingness. And he knew worse was to come, but he had to let it play out. He knew the sound of the argument would never leave him, the angry, bitter words, cousin against cousin, both men dangerously in love with Ella Carrick.

Adam had Jacob on the ground now; he was taller and stronger, the punches becoming more aggressive. Jacob, pinned down on his back, groped around the area, looking for something to defend himself with, something to get Adam off him. His fingers found a rock and closed over it; he brought the rock up, slamming it into the side of Adam's head. There was a gasp and Adam's *eyes opened wide. Then he went limp and fell, tumbling away from Jacob and lying motionless in the mud . . .*

Ned swore and slammed his fist into the hand-rail. This was his cross to bear. This. The fact he had to stand back and watch it happen. The fact he couldn't help them; the fact he had gone there, and broken all the rules by doing so. He raised his head, his cheeks damp — but whether it was tears, sea-spray or snow, he didn't know and he didn't care.

'I know there's never an easy way!' he shouted into the darkness. 'I know it had to happen — but . . . ' He listened, as if someone would answer him. Nobody did. 'Why them? Why *them*?' Silence answered him and he shook his head. 'I know. I know.' His voice broke and he stared at the ground again, his eyes tracing the edge of the cliff, black on black. 'I shouldn't have been there, I should have stayed away. But I couldn't. I just couldn't. I hoped it would be different.' He looked up again and trained his gaze on the vast, lonely horizon. 'But it never is, is it?'

A soft hand laid itself on top of his, with just enough pressure to let him know she was there. He didn't look in her direction. He didn't try to see her.

It wasn't the first time he had felt her near him, but he was surprised she was here and he just nodded. 'I would have stopped it if I could,' he told her. 'You know that, don't you? Nobody who knew you properly could fail to love you in some way, but you were always his. And I'm sorry. I'm so sorry.'

He didn't expect an answer. Could she even hear what he was saying? But apparently, she understood. She squeezed his hand and a kiss as soft as a whisper touched his cheek.

'So I take it I'm forgiven?' he asked, smiling crookedly. Another squeeze of his hand confirmed that. 'I should go to her. I shouldn't wait, should I? I don't want to waste any more time.' He looked up into the clouds as they parted across the moon, marking out a silver channel through the sea. He followed the glittering pathway and saw it led onto the jagged rocks below. He shuddered and looked back up at the moon. 'I still wonder what you told her that Christmas Eve we were all together, when you were alone with her in the drawing room. She wouldn't tell me. I know you said something, something in that way you had, something only the two of you understood. I should have learned your language — I might have eavesdropped.'

A breeze wafted past him, and it seemed as if the wind whispered in his ear: *I said enough.*

'Enough,' he repeated. He nodded again. Then he narrowed his eyes and looked along the cliff path. A shadowy figure, darker even than the velvet sky stood patiently. 'I can see he's waiting for you. Go to him. You've always been his angel and after all it's Christmas — everyone needs their angels at Christmas.'

There was a breath of wind that may

or may not have been a giggle, and he felt the hand lift from his. He waited a few seconds, then looked back at the cliff path; for a moment, the moon-shadows shifted and changed and he saw her next to him; saw her tilt her head up and kiss him. Then he took her hand and there was nothing else to be seen, and Ned knew he was alone again.

8

Christmas Night

The final couple walked out of the room, shouting thanks to Ailsa over their shoulders and she followed them, closing the double doors firmly on the stragglers. Almost immediately, the drawing room seemed to settle and she leaned her forehead on the wood, closing her eyes and just enjoying the silence.

Half of her expected to hear the notes of *O Holy Night* drifting through the room, but of course that wouldn't happen. Even if Ella *did* play Christmas carols as a break from Mozart, she wouldn't play them when anyone was in the room. She was a notoriously private ghost, at least as far as showing herself to Carrick Park staff was concerned.

Ailsa turned the key in the lock, and walked back into the drawing room. It was almost midnight and Christmas Day was ending. She always felt a little deflated when Christmas Day was over; the magic of Christmas Eve had long since vanished and, to be honest, this Christmas Day had been much like any other working day. Although she loved her job, she couldn't help feeling just a little bit resentful that she'd had no time to herself. Oh well. It had been better than sitting on her own all day, overdosing on chocolates and Christmas pudding. And maybe next year nobody would want to get married on the twenty-fifth and she'd have somewhere to go and someone to spend Christmas with properly.

She went over to the piano and tutted as she saw that someone had left a champagne glass on it. No — *two* people had left their glasses and she felt aggrieved on Ella's behalf. It wasn't the original piano, but still — it was just laziness. The dying fire flickered gold across the piano and, as the light glinted off another object, she noticed something else.

A soft-bodied, china-faced angel with silver wings lay there, next to a sprig of mistletoe. It looked very much like the one from Lydia's tree. Ailsa picked the little creature up and turned it in her hands. It must have come off the tree in the hallway — that was clearly how it had found its way into her dream last night. It had to be a dream. It had to be. She sighed as she laid the angel back down, and made to pick up the glasses and put them on a table.

Almost unnoticed, a gentle breeze drifted across the room and Ailsa's skin prickled.

'Merry Christmas, Ailsa. I hope you liked your gift. She's travelled a long way, relatively speaking.'

She spun around, and he was there, in front of the French doors. The filmy material moved a little, but there was no sign that he'd come in that way — no sign of the doors opening, no sign that he'd somehow managed to unlock the main doors and sneak up on her; nothing.

'Ned!'

The room was suddenly filled with a crackling energy that had nothing to do with the flames leaping up merrily in the fireplace. He took a few steps towards her, and she mirrored his movements. They met, somewhere in the middle of the room and Ailsa felt sure her heart would gallop right out of her body. His eyes met hers, so dark, they were almost black. Golden flecks from the flames reflected in them and his face, half in shadow, looked strained. His back was to the French doors, and, beyond him, she could see the gardens sparkling with a hoar frost, as if someone had tossed a tub of glitter over the shrubbery.

She reached out a hand and, almost without thinking, laid it on his chest. He felt warm and solid and very much alive.

'Are you real, Ned?' she asked, the question sounding silly in the warm, wintery room.

Ned laughed, the sound as soft as a snowflake. 'Why wouldn't I be?' His face relaxed and his gaze travelled all over her, as if he was checking that she too was real.

'Because — ' She stopped, thinking how odd it would all sound. *Because you just appear and disappear at random; because you took me to Carrick Park in 1864; because you knew the Carrick family; because they said you went there every Christmas. Because you made me think you wouldn't come back until* next *Christmas.* 'Just — because,' she finished weakly.

'I'm real enough,' he said. 'I just couldn't wait until next Christmas to see you again. Maybe I'm going to get into trouble for coming back so soon, maybe I should have stayed away for a little longer, like I was supposed to do; but when you know, you know, don't you? And you don't *want* to have to wait. Sometimes, you just need to grab that moment. I needed to grab that moment with you; I need to have longer with you. I need forever.' Her hand was still resting on his chest and he covered it with his; then he gently lifted it away and up to his lips. He brushed it with a kiss and pulled her towards him. He tenderly placed his other hand on her waist, so she was close to him — so very close — and she was looking up at him, unable to shift her gaze from his eyes. 'My life is a bit different to yours. There are places I go; places I need to go to. Places I've been and don't want to go back to.' His eyes darkened for a moment. 'I've got a job to do and sometimes it's hard.'

'What do you mean?' asked Ailsa.

'I mean,' he replied, smiling sadly, 'that I can't always help people. Just like I told you. Sometimes, you just have to let things happen, even though it goes against your very nature. And sometimes you fall for people, just a little bit, and you know that you have to step back. It's not your decision to make.'

Ailsa looked at him, trying to read the meaning in his face. 'Like Ella,' she said suddenly. 'When I mentioned her and how I wished I could warn her. You said not to do that.'

'Exactly like Ella.'

'You could have saved her — you could have warned her. If we were really there — '

'We *were* really there,' he interrupted softly. 'Don't doubt that at all.'

Ailsa thought she would collapse and Ned held her more tightly, shoring her up, almost. None of this made any sense; she couldn't even believe she was saying such things. She was probably dreaming again. The warmth of the room and the exhaustion had finally hit her and she had dozed off . . .

'But why? Why couldn't you tell her?' her voice seemed to be coming from very far away.

'What could I say? 'Come away with me, Ella. I'll look after you. I'll make sure you're safe.' I couldn't do that. To do that, I would have had to rip her away from Adam and there was never anybody else for either of them. There never will be. They were soulmates, it's

179

as simple as that. I loved her, in my own way — how could anyone not love Ella — but he was born for her. Just like I was born for someone else.'

'Soulmates.' Ailsa whispered the word. 'I guess I'm in that sort of business too — I try to make sure they have the best start to it all. I deal with people in love every day.'

'So do I, much of the time. I have to make sure people are in the right place, at the right time. I have to make sure the wheels are in motion. And I had to take you to that particular Christmas, because there was never another like it, not after what happened. Not after she died.' He stared into the distance, as if he was seeing it all again. 'I didn't go the next year, the year after it all happened. It had only been a couple of months, and the family were in mourning anyway, but I had a good excuse not to go. I went after that, but it was never the same. As I said to you yesterday, what was the point of letting them know? They might as well have

180

enjoyed the time they had together and they did.'

'But what keeps her here?' Ailsa's eyes drifted over to the piano, where the little angel was now, somehow, propped up against one of the glasses. 'The angel! She's moved!'

Ned laughed. 'She has. Maybe it was Ella. Look, I think there's something else there too. Come on.' He took her hand and led her over to the piano. 'And in answer to your question, I suspect it's love that keeps her here. Love for the Park, love for Adam and probably, knowing Ella, a love for her piano. Ah, here we go. Perfect.'

He reached over and produced a bottle of champagne that was sitting in an ice-bucket, just behind the piano, out of sight.

'That's from the wedding party!' protested Ailsa. 'You can't have that.'

Ned turned to her, a twinkle in his eye. 'Wrong brand. Look.' He held the bottle out, and she saw that it was indeed a different sort to what the happy couple and their guests had been merrily swigging all day. In fact, it wasn't even a brand the hotel sold.

'How on earth . . . ?'

'Nothing to do with earth,' replied Ned with a wink. 'Now — shall we?'

'The glasses — '

' — are ours,' he continued. 'Not left over from the party at all. I promise you.' He popped the cork and upended the bottle, filling the glasses for them. He held one out to Ailsa and she took it, hesitating only briefly before taking a drink. It was awfully good champagne, she had to give whoever had provided it credit for that.

'How did you get in here?' she asked him. 'And how did you get the angel and the champagne?'

'I'm just going to claim it was another little bit of Christmas magic,' he replied with a grin. He raised the glass and toasted her. 'To us. And to Christmas. To all of our Christmases — especially the Carrick Park ones.'

'The Carrick Park ones?' Ailsa knew

she sounded dim, but it felt absolutely surreal. Why, if she half-closed her eyes, there was a Christmas tree, with a bent-over top, wavering just out of focus. If she turned to face it — it was gone.

'Did you see it?' asked Ned, following her gaze. 'The tree? Yes — the Carrick Park Christmases. This one, here and now, and the other one. The one you wished for on Christmas Eve.'

'I saw the tree. But you left me. You took me to the *other* Carrick Park, and you brought me back — then you left me! It wasn't much of a Christmas here, was it?'

'I completely agree — which is why I wanted to spend longer with you. What we did and the time we had here just wasn't enough. I did leave — but then I found there was something worth coming back for. I didn't want to wait until next year. Maybe I should have done; by rights, I should have done. You're not supposed to rush these things — even though I was desperate to start the next part of our lives. I think seeing Ella and Adam brought it home to me. It didn't take me long to decide I had to turn around and come back for you. When you know, you know. As I told you.'

He smiled down at her and she was drowning in those eyes again. 'When you know what?'

'When you know you've found your someone — your soulmate — the person you were born for.'

'Ned!'

'I know — it's safe for me to tell you all this, though, because you won't remember it. I can tell you anything. I can tell you that I love you and it tears me apart whenever I have to leave you. Always has done, always will do.'

'But we barely know each other. We spent one day together!'

'One perfect day.' He refilled her glass. 'Go on, enjoy it. Before you forget. We'll have other days, though — lots of them.'

'I'm not going to forget — '

Ned nodded. 'You are, my love,

because it has to be that way. You wish on an angel and the wishes are as fragile as their wings. They're real, but not real. It's weird — even now, after so long, I find it hard to explain.' He laughed and took her hand, rubbing the soft pad of her thumb with his. The touch, combined with the second glass of champagne was enough to make her legs go wobbly. And immediately, the whole scenario seemed rather — normal. She was meant to be in here, with him, sipping champagne and talking about angels.

'An angel?' she managed. 'My china angel? That one?'

'If that's the one you think you wished on, then yes, that one.'

Ailsa opened her mouth to respond, then checked herself.

She took a deep breath and tried again. 'I didn't have the china angel when I wished I could spend Christmas with Lydia and Ella,' she said quietly.

'So you didn't,' replied Ned, just as quietly. He took the glass out of her hand and placed it carefully on the table next to his.

'There was just you in the room. Just you and me.'

'Very true.'

'So what are you trying to say?'

'What are *you* trying to say?'

'I — '

But the words were lost as he leaned down and kissed her. 'What was that?' he teased as he pulled away.

'What *are* you?' Ailsa asked, searching his face for an answer.

'I'm yours for as long as we live,' he replied, his eyes amused.

'I don't understand,' she said, lost.

'Can't you feel it? In here?' he asked. He placed her fingers on his chest, just over where his heart was beating.

As he pressed her hand against his body, all sorts of images began to flood into her mind — images of things they'd done or things they were going to do. Times they'd shared, but hadn't yet shared. Laughter and tears, now, in the future, in the past; and a deep, deep abiding love that was as firm as the ground they were standing on, as solid as the walls of this old house they both loved.

'How?' she whispered. 'How is that happening?'

'One word. If you had one word to describe it, what would you say?'

His voice was hypnotic, and she felt compelled to answer: 'Soulmates.'

'Soulmates,' he replied. 'You're right. *That's* what happens. We've found each other again, like we always do. And that's the way it works in your world as well. I just have to split my time between our two worlds, which is always the problem. Like I said, I hate leaving you.'

'But — if this is real — if it *is* real — what if you have to go away again? What'll happen?'

Ned grinned. 'In your world, I'll be the sort of boyfriend who has to work away a lot. You'll think I'm doing a normal sort of job, but really I'll be doing this. You won't remember any of this conversation at all. And that's something I have to deal with — all the time, all through our lives. I love this bit, though. I love to see your face when you realise.'

'I don't quite know what I'm realising,' replied Ailsa. The champagne really had gone to her head — the whole room was getting fuzzy and she was finding it difficult to focus on him. 'I don't want to forget this Christmas. I don't want to forget all about the Carricks and the ice-skating and the Lord and Lady of Misrule. Or this. Having champagne with you, seeing my little china angel.' The panic crept into her voice.

'You'll not forget, not properly. It'll be just like a dream — a really vivid dream; the sort you want to escape into, the sort you remember time after time. It'll always be there. You'll just think you dreamed it all, with me in it. You already told me I've appeared in your dreams. That's why — this has all happened before for us, and you're simply remembering fragments of our lives.'

188

Ailsa shook her head, trying to put it all together. 'Can you tell me one thing, though.' She blinked and stood up straighter, determined not to slump into an inelegant heap on the floor. 'If you had a life then — and if I was part of it — if I was Ailsa Cavendish, like we pretended — then what happened to me? How did you explain my disappearance — the disappearance of the version of me that was there? If I *did* disappear? People didn't really get divorced too often then, did they? And I'm worried that you told them I'd died or something. Or maybe I *did* die! Good Lord. I'm confusing myself.'

Ned laughed and pulled her closer; he steadied her and kissed her, and smiled into her eyes. 'None of those things happened. Do you want to know why we didn't go to Carrick Park the year Ella died? Why I had a good excuse not to go?'

Ailsa nodded, entranced at the story, determined that, whatever he did to her, she would never forget any of this.

'Well, my love. We didn't go, because you were just about to give birth to our first son.' Ned's eyes twinkled. 'A bonny lad, he was, born on Christmas Day, as it happens. And he grew up happy and strong and healthy, in a muddle of siblings. There was no better reason to stay at home, really.'

Ailsa stared at him. 'So we were really married? We stayed married? And we had children together?'

'We did,' said Ned with a smile. 'We always do.' He raised his hand and tucked a lock of hair behind her ear. 'Like I said to you, some people are just born for one another. They find their soulmates in whatever life they lead — but they don't always recognise them straight away. Unless you've got a job like mine, in which case you kind of know certain things. And I sort of help things along.'

'So we've been together before,' Ailsa said slowly, trying to make sense of it all.

'We've already lived a few lives together,' replied Ned softly. 'You only saw a little part of one of them. One day, I might take you back to another one. But for now, I think we have to concentrate on this one.' He moved his hand, tracing his fingers down her cheekbone. 'I have to do it. I'm sorry. But I do love you, and I'll always come back to you. Remember that. When you wake up, you'll just remember that we met and chatted on Christmas Eve, and I was perhaps a guest at the wedding, hovering somewhere in the background. Then afterwards, I came and found you, and handed you a little china angel that I thought must have fallen off the tree. But you kept it, because they'd never put china angels on the tree, and the rest followed after that, as natural as breathing. It just felt right — you knew we were meant for one another. And so we are, and so we will be.'

His voice was soft and lulling her into a daydream; a daydream where she was skating on a frozen lake, and his arms were wrapped around her and they were both terrible at it. And Adam Carrick was picking Ella Dunbar off the ground because she'd slipped, and Lydia Carrick was laughing fit to burst over their antics . . . *You're hereafter known as the Lord and Lady of Misrule!* she declared, and Adam shouted *Whatever do you mean by that . . .*

Ailsa's mind began to drift, as it did just before she fell into a deep sleep, and she felt her whole body relax. She was vaguely aware of being picked up in his arms and felt a gentle kiss brush her forehead before the darkness and the silence all around claimed her.

Then she was in bed, in the midst of the most delicious dream she'd ever had.

Boxing Day

The alarm clock woke her at seven, and Ailsa stretched, rolled over and saw the china angel on the bedside table, sitting on top of the book about Carrick Park.

She wondered for a moment what it was doing there — it was a funny little thing, very sweet with a soft body and silver wings. Then she remembered and she began to smile. Ned. The guy from the wedding party last night. He'd given her it, hadn't he? Nobody recognised it as one from the Carrick Park tree, so Ailsa had brought it upstairs and claimed it as her own.

Her mobile phone was blinking as well, and she pulled it towards her to read the message:

Are you around for breakfast? I am. Fancy sharing a table?

Ailsa laughed and began to type a response.

Good morning, Ned. Yes, I'm here. See you at eight?

Sounds good to me, he responded.

Yes, Ailsa thought as she stretched and sat up. Working Christmas Day hadn't really been too bad, all things considered. It meant, at the very least, she could spend some of Boxing Day with a dark haired, dark-eyed man called Ned, who she very much wanted to get to know a whole lot better . . .

9

Christmas Yet to Come

One Year Later

'Is Ned definitely going to make it back for Christmas then?' Tara was clicking half-heartedly through the bookings screen.

Tara had, as far as she was concerned, drawn the short straw — she *wasn't* working the rest of Christmas Eve, so she would, she had moaned, have to put up with the family stresses instead. She was just getting ready to hand over to Louisa, and Ailsa was keeping her company for a little while before going home herself.

'He should make it,' agreed Ailsa. 'He was caught up with some IT job in the Highlands, but he promised me he'd be back. So I believe him. He's never let me down yet.'

'I bet you're pleased you don't have any weddings tomorrow. It was hard work last year, wasn't it?' Tara pulled a face, then dragged a plate with the remnants of a slice of Christmas cake on it closer to her. 'Rosa's going to make me fat. Honestly, they'll be stuffing me and putting me on the table for Christmas dinner.'

'It was hard work, but it had a decent outcome. I wouldn't have met Ned otherwise. Anyway, did Rosa tell you that she and Joel are heading to Cornwall in the New Year? I can think of warmer places to visit, but there you go. She might make us scones when she comes back.' Ailsa broke off a piece of her own cake and popped it into her mouth, one eye on the main doors. 'She'll more than likely come back pregnant, though. I've warned her.'

Tara laughed. 'That's kind of you!'

Ailsa grinned. 'It wasn't me, it was Ned. Can you remember when she brought her niece in to see us, when her sister Jessie was up at Staithes for something to do with her bookshop?'

'Ah! Lottie. Yes, she was a cutie.'

'Ned said then. He said 'Oh, there's a twinkle in her eye — she'll have one of her own by next Christmas.''

'And you believed him?' Tara shook her head and continued demolishing the cake. She pressed the last few crumbs together into a little wodge and finished them off, licking her fingers, just to make sure.

'He's rarely wrong. I mean *you* for instance — '

'Stop it!' Tara held up her hand. 'No thanks. I don't want to know!'

'Okay. Fair enough.'

Ailsa was just about to continue the conversation, when a gentle breeze wrapped itself around her legs and shivered up her spine. She knew without even looking that he had come, just as he'd promised.

'Ned!' Sure enough, as she turned to face the main doors, she saw they were opening. Ned came through them, blown in on a light flurry of snow. He paused, kicking the slush off his boots, diamond sparkles in his dark hair as the snowflakes settled and melted and disappeared.

'Hey gorgeous!' he said, opening his arms wide.

'You made it!' cried Ailsa, hurrying over to meet him. She fitted into his arms and he kissed her, his nose cold but his lips warm on hers. 'The roads are okay then?'

'The roads are fine,' he said. 'And of course I made it. I'll always be back for Christmas, never worry about that.'

'Always?' she teased him, brushing some snow off his shoulders. Beyond him, the snow was lying in the gardens, and Ailsa thought about all the Christmases that Carrick Park had known. She recalled the dream she'd had again last night, the one about ice-skating near the Abbey and Ella playing carols in the drawing room. It must have been a special sort of place. It still was a special sort of place.

She blushed as she recalled the second part of the dream; the part where the scenery had changed and she was mistress of a big old Georgian house she thought was possibly up in Edinburgh. In that dream, her stomach was as round and as hard as a football, and Ned was kissing her as he pressed his hand against her bump, and she covered his hand with hers and together they marvelled over the whole thing.

She didn't think she'd ever dare tell him that one — or the fact that in her half-waking, half-dozing sleep, she could almost swear she'd felt the baby kicking and stretching around inside of her. She had been thrown when she woke up, just as slim as she usually was, and certainly not in a big old house in Edinburgh.

'You know I'll always come back to you,' said Ned. He caught her hand in his and kissed it, pulling her closer to him. 'I'll *always* be back for Christmas — for the rest of our lives.'

It was a warming thought. Ailsa

snuggled into him, closing her eyes and inhaling the scent of winter and frost and pine that clung to his overcoat. She imagined a Christmas with Carrick Park blanketed in a carpet of white, and she and Ned kissing beneath a sprig of mistletoe, her china angel glimmering in the candlelight of a huge, ill-fitting tree.

And somewhere, perhaps in a waking dream, or perhaps in reality, the last few notes of *O Holy Night* drifted across the hallway and died away with the sound of the breeze.